BL: 5.1 -
AR PLS: 4.0
Quiz No. 505164

D042670-4

FOL

Other books by Obert Skye

Geeked Out

THE CREATURE FROM MY CLOSET SERIES:

Wonkenstein

Potterwookiee

Pinocula

Katfish

The Lord of the Hat

Batneezer

THE WITHERWOOD REFORM SCHOOL SERIES:

Witherwood Reform School

Lost & Found

OBERT SKYE

Geeked Out Book 2

Christy Ottaviano Books

HENRY HOLT AND COMPANY

NEW YORK

Henry Holt and Company, *Publishers since 1866*
Henry Holt® is a registered trademark of Macmillan Publishing Group, LLC
175 Fifth Avenue, New York, NY 10010
mackids.com

Library of Congress Control Number: 2018945024
ISBN 978-1-62779-941-6

Our books may be purchased in bulk for promotional, educational, or
business use. Please contact your local bookseller or the Macmillan Corporate
and Premium Sales Department at (800) 221-7945 ext. 5442 or by email at
MacmillanSpecialMarkets@macmillan.com.

First edition, 2019 / Designed by Carol Ly

Printed in the United States of America by LSC Communications,
Harrisonburg, Virginia

1   3   5   7   9   10   8   6   4   2

To David, the funniest, nerdiest,
perfect little brother.
Sorry about breaking your airplane.

Contents

CHAPTER ONE

Otto Waddle Jr. High Outpost

You'd think that I'd be happy. After all, for the first time in my life, I have some good things going on. Sure, the world is falling apart more each day, but my own life has a few positives.

For one, I am still president of the AV Club. AV used to stand for Audio Visual but now it stands for Avoid Violence. That's just because of the whole "world falling apart" thing.

I also have some pretty good friends. Like me, they're members of the AV Club, and we've been through a lot together. There are four of us: me, Mindy, Owen, and Xennitopher. The *me* in that last sentence is me, Tip. My actual name is Timothy Dover, but I used to have a difficult time walking and managing gravity, which meant I fell occasionally. And since my real name sounds a lot like *tipped over,* everyone began calling me Tip. Tip Dover. I tried to explain that the reason I fell over was because my brain was so big it made me lopsided, but that still didn't stop anyone from teasing me. In fact, a few people now call me Fat Brain.

My friends and I have always gotten along. We share the common trait of being geeks and outcasts. Now we have an even bigger connection. There is something that makes us vastly different than before. It's not our hair or our IQs, because those things have always been high. The difference is that we now have super . . . well, we have powers.

Say what?

What.

2

Our abilities may not be as flashy as the ones you see in comic books, but they are powers nonetheless. And together we used our gifts to save our school from extinction. It wasn't easy, but we pulled it off.

Since then we have helped save a few things around the city—cats stuck in trees, kids chased by drones, and people being picked on by Fanatics. Despite all the things we have done for Piggsburg, nobody at our school knows it's us who keep saving the day. We are a mysterious, supersecret group called the League of Average and Mediocre Entities, or LAME. Laugh if you want, but we even have outfits that help us hide our identities and partial awesomeness.

Mindy can clap and cause damage to almost anything. Xen has powerful burps that can knock things down.

Owen can hear like a freak, but now he struggles hearing sounds that are close. Me? Well, I can turn almost anything on and off just by thinking about it. We're still the same nerdy AV Club members we once were, but now LAME has a little street cred.

POWER:
Deadly claps
WEAKNESS:
Unknown

THE CLAPPER

BELCH BOY

POWER:
Burps of
destruction
WEAKNESS:
Illogical
people

POWERS:
Superhearing,
glowing eyes
WEAKNESS:
Pudding

EYES + EARS

WONDER NERD

POWER:
Can start or
stop any
machine or
electronic
device at will
WEAKNESS:
Sweaty pits

Sure, we could go around telling the world who we are and all about our maddish skillz, but as anyone who has ever picked up a comic book knows, semi-superheroes don't do that.

Besides, if we give away our secrets, the world would become even more dangerous and unsettling for us. Our families would be targeted, and the government would lock us up and perform all kinds of tests on us.

For the record, things used to be okay. Planet Earth was once holding its own. In fact, when I was a kid, life was almost normal. Then a few years ago, things started to change. Pollution was out of control, cities were overcrowded, and wars became a daily occurrence. Then things went from really bad to really awful. The event that pushed society over the edge was the release of the third Sand Thrower movie: *Grainy*.

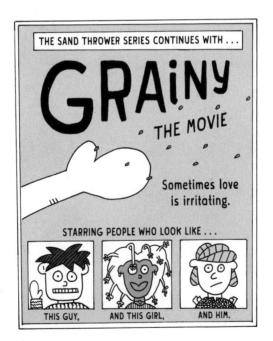

Normally, movies don't change the world, but this one did. See, the Sand Thrower series is a popular book series. Every girl and lots of boys love it. They talk endlessly about the characters, the story, and the covers.

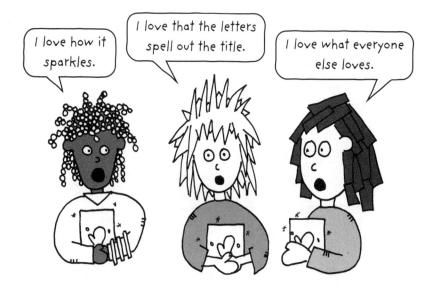

Personally, I think the books are horrible. I don't mean to rip books apart for no reason, so here are some reasons:

I'd rather read a book about stomach worms and the bacteria they digest. But the rest of the world feels differently. That's why when Hollywood made the third Sand Thrower book into a movie and that movie blew chunks, the entire planet went nuts.

The fans of the series left the theaters, took to the streets, and began to terrorize everyone. They disrupted society so much that cities began to crack under the stress. The fans—or

Fanatics, as they became known—stormed the companies that endorsed the third movie. They marched in the streets in anger. Their anger tore apart towns. Their postings and rantings on social media were so great that communications satellites couldn't handle the overload and fell from the skies. The falling satellites caused other satellites to fall. With so many satellites down, factories went off-line and began to mistakenly pump out more pollution than ever before. The pollution caused the weather to get worse, and the conditions caused the entire world to go to war. These days everything is a war—oxygen wars, tax wars, walking wars, pudding wars.

With all the chaos and turmoil, the United States of America went from being fifty united states to being seventy-three Somewhat United, Sort of Divided States of America. Countries fell apart and regrouped under different names. Some of the names were based on the horrible film that began it all. Italy was now called Utterly, because the movie was utterly awful. Germany was now called Das Third Movie Stunk.

Things were bad.

And through it all, the angry and disappointed Fanatics continue to take to the streets each night and terrorize everyone.

So nothing is normal anymore. Food is hard to come by, no place feels safe, and middle school is worse than ever.

My school is Otto Waddle Jr. High Government Outpost. We call it WADD for short because it's kind of a big wad of confusion. It's old and in bad shape, and as underfunded as most places in the town of Piggsburg.

Like so many middle schools, it's filled with normal cliques like Jocks and Geeks and Goths and Cheerleaders. But because everyone needs a group to survive these days, there are way more unusual cliques: Sox, Pens, Loners, Loaners, Antisocials, Old-Timers, Sci-Fis, Wi-Fis, and many others. Even the teachers are a group called the Staffers.

The school day can be dangerous, and the Staffers seem more frightened of the students than we are of them. It's students against Staffers every day in some sort of Supply War or Homework War or administrative battle.

WADD is a school on the brink of disaster.

Our principal is Hyrum Woth. He is a coward and rarely does anything other than hide. Principal Woth's only goal is to make sure nobody can ask him for help. He also doesn't want to make any decisions or face any responsibility. Woth is supposed to be our leader, but he hardly runs the school.

The person who runs everything at WADD is the school secretary, Mrs. Susan. For the record, she's not nice. Also, if someone is keeping a second record, let me just say that she is SO NOT nice that she's evil. Plus, her hair smells like decaying lettuce.

Mrs. Susan sits on top of her pile of desks in the front office, smiling insincerely and telling everyone what to do.

She makes daily announcements through the broken intercom system, which causes her voice to sound like Darth Vader's.

We call her Darth Susan, but only behind her back, because if she found out, she would send us to the detention compound behind the school and make us spend our afternoons busting up rocks. She usually sounds kind of fake-sweet, but lately she just sounds real-sad.

Bless my sad heart. I just don't feel up to being cruel.

I'm guessing that anyone reading this book is smart, and because you are smart, you're probably asking yourself, *Why would anyone bother saving a school as horrible as Otto Waddle?* Well, it may seem hard to believe, but there are far worse schools out there. For example, outpost #72. It's where we would have all been sent if our school had been closed. Outpost #72 is located on the edge of Piggsburg and includes all the troubled students and a few ex-cons. The halls are filled with social-networking gangs that bully everyone, and their mascot is a fist that runs around punching things.

So, as awful as WADD can be, we still prefer it over the other option. And ever since we saved the place, Darth Susan has been depressed. She hardly has the energy to boss kids around.

To cheer her up, Tyler, the school janitor, built her a Hall-Terrain-Vehicle, or HTV, out of scraps and pieces of things he had scavenged from the garbage wasteland on the east end of town.

The HTV didn't seem to cheer her up.

But last week things seemed to change.

On Tuesday, Darth Susan wasn't at school. On Wednesday, she returned and seemed to be back to her old rotten self. Once again she was terrorizing the halls and scaring us all with her sickeningly sweet way of making threats.

The evil glint in her eyes had returned, and as everyone knows, an evil glint is the worst kind of glint there is. Something had happened on her day off—something that had changed things and now threatened to ruin our short run of semi-peace. If Darth Susan was happy again, that meant bad things were on the horizon. She had even bought a daily cruel-planner and was carrying it around everywhere she went.

Due to her change of black heart and the return of her evildoing, we were already on edge and on the verge of feeling awful. But to make things feel even worse, five minutes before school was to let out, the speakers clicked to life so that Darth Susan could make one final announcement.

Before you all leave for the day, I have one last thing to say. I know that for the past two months there have been rumors and spottings of this group called LAME. If anyone sees them, please take pictures. You will receive extra credit. I want to be able to thank them personally. That is all.

Something was wrong. Darth Susan had never mentioned our name. Now she was asking people to be on the lookout for us. There was trouble afoot, and afoot trouble is almost as bad as abutt trouble.

LAME had some investigating to do.

The four of us had been working on a tagline for our group. Something we could yell when we were on the case or saving the world. So far we had come up with . . .

We could hear Finn the school crier crying out. Thanks to all the uncertainty in the world, only the government can set off alarms or bells. So our school uses Finn. He cries out when school periods end, or when the day is over, or when there's information that Darth Susan doesn't want to squawk about herself.

The school day was over, and everyone raced to get as far away from WADD as possible. Everyone except for us.

CHAPTER TWO

Sending Ourselves to the Office

We gathered in the Geek Cave after school. It's not really a cave. It's more like a small, hidden room behind one of the cabinets in the school cafeteria.

It was also the place where we had been bitten by the spiders that had given us our abilities. They were spiders that had been soaking in some sort of Salisbury steak for thirty years. When we opened the can, they poured out by the hundreds and munched on us.

It was dark in the Geek Cave, as usual, so Owen turned on his eyes. We sat around and discussed what we needed to do about Darth Susan. She was acting cruel again and looking for us. It was not a good combination.

"Why would she want people to take pictures of us?" Xen asked. "Is she getting into scrapbooking and she wants to preserve the memory of the people who defeated her?"

"We'll figure this out," Mindy said.

I couldn't see clearly, but I'm pretty sure Mindy was smiling at me. We sort of have a history. It's complicated, but I'll tell you this: Three days ago things really started to heat up. We accidentally held hands while I was giving her a flash drive she needed. My reply was far from smooth.

Sitting in the Geek Cave, we asked Owen if he could hear Darth Susan talking wherever she was.

"No," Owen replied. "I've tried, but the only thing I ever hear is her talking to her lizard. And I don't like listening to that for too long."

Darth Susan's lizard is named Becky, and she treats it like her child. She also lets it roam all over WADD as a hall monitor of sorts.

Becky bites people's ankles if they're late to class and smears lizard poop all over the floors and walls with her feet. Sure, it's not like our school is going to win any awards for beauty, but adding lizard poop to the mix doesn't help.

"So, what should we do?" Xen asked.

I know! We can use our powers to amass great wealth. Then we'll build a fortress on top of a mountain, where we can look down at everyone and rule over the very people who have bullied us our whole lives.

"Instead," Mindy suggested, "let's try to find Darth Susan's cruel-planner and see if there are any answers inside. Either it's in the school office or she took it home."

"Is the school empty?" I asked Owen.

He listened for a second. "I can hear Tyler snoring out back by the shelter tables. Judging by the sound of a motor running, I'd say he's napping on the HTV."

We left the Geek Cave and pushed the cabinet back into place to hide the opening. The cafeteria was dark, but I could see two stray dogs sniffing around under one of the tables. The city of Piggsburg was filled with wild animals. Almost every afternoon, dogs would come in through the security hole and scrounge around our school for any food that might have been dropped in the cafeteria.

My three friends followed me out of the cafeteria and down the main hall. It was late afternoon now. Through the windows, I could see that the sky outside was filled with large dust clouds, causing things to be darker than usual.

We got to the office with no difficulty. (The door was locked, which didn't surprise any of us.) So Mindy clapped to bust the doorknob but instead the bottom half of the door cracked and fell to the floor.

We crawled into the dark office, and Owen lit things up with his eyes. Quickly, we searched the office looking for Darth Susan's black cruel-planner. I turned on her computer with my mind to see if there was any info there. The only thing that stood out was a flash drive that was labeled VACATION PHOTOS. I shivered thinking about what was on that.

We checked all the stacked desks, but there was no sign of her cruel-planner.

Wait, I can hear some people moving around the front of the school.

"Fanatics?" Mindy said, shivering.

"No," Owen replied.

"Then, who?" Xen asked nervously.

Sure, we were superheroes, but we were also mortal, with the same scaredy-cat gene that everyone has. Usually people didn't hang around WADD after school ended. The moment Finn the crier cries out, everyone bails as fast as possible.

The government also doesn't like people standing around on the streets if it isn't necessary. Everyone is supposed to go home directly after school or work and stay hunkered until (if and when) the next day ever comes. It's dangerous to be on the streets when the world is full of Fanatics who swarm you and pick you apart until you have no self-esteem or desire to go on.

Owen could still hear people out in front of WADD.

"If they're not Fanatics, who are they?" Mindy asked. "Half-Deads?"

"I don't think so," Owen answered. "Half-Deads never laugh, and these people are laughing."

The four of us crawled under the broken door and out of Darth Susan's office. Owen turned off his eyes, and we held our breath to listen for any sound from outside.

"Whoever it is, they're near the security hole," Owen whispered.

The security hole was near the chained front doors. All the students and Staffers had to crawl through the hole to enter the school. The small size allowed people to get through, but not tanks or cars or bazookas. The hole was always open, which made it easy for tiny animals or regular-sized people to slip in and out whenever they wanted to. It was supposed to make us feel safe, but it was just an open hole.

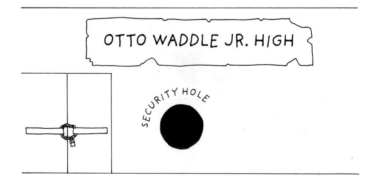

I saw a shadow pass in front of the security hole.

All four of us backed up against the lockers on the opposite side of the hall, away from the hole.

One after another, four shadows slipped into the school and stood up in the dark hall. I couldn't tell who they were because it was dark and they looked like nothing but shadows. The person closest to us spoke.

The voice was off a little, but I could tell it was Nerf. He was the leader of the Jocks and the worst person at WADD after Darth Susan. Nerf and his friends loved giving us a hard time.

"I asked you a question," Nerf continued. "Nobody should be in here."

It was too dark to see his face or the face of any of the other three.

"We—" I started to say.

"Are in trouble!" he yelled.

Fighting Nerf with our abilities would have given away our secret identities, so we quickly took off and ran down Q Hall.

"Get them!" Nerf yelled.

We raced down the hall and spun around the corner, toward the library.

It was a dumb move.

Everybody knows that the library is a dead end. Not only is it located at the end of D Hall, but the librarian, Mrs. Shh, always keeps it locked to prevent any students from coming in and bothering her.

Leave my realm before I am forced to start throwing books.

She was not a librarian to be trifled with. Not only was she frightening, she had also invented the Very Dismal System. It was a way to never locate the books you wanted. The system was so confusing that even Xen's brilliant coding mind couldn't crack it. He had tried, but he always ended up passing out.

It was a shame that our library was trying to keep me out because I like to read. My favorite things are manuals and instruction books. It's comforting to me to understand how things work. I also enjoy reading information on the internet and visiting sites like Clickapedia. But books are the best way for me to cram my head with things that other people don't even know about.

We reached the library doors, and Owen tried to pull them open. As we'd expected, they were locked. I heard Nerf and his dim-witted friends running down Q Hall and getting closer.

Knowing Nerf couldn't see us, Mindy clapped. I'm not sure what she was hoping to do, but the hinges on the library doors cracked and burst. The four of us jumped forward and slammed into the doors. They fell over and crashed against the floor. Xen went down with them, so I reached out to pull him up.

Leave me!
Save yourself!

"No way!"

"What's Nerf doing here?" he screamed.

I pulled Xen up without answering, and we ran into the library after Mindy and Owen.

A lot of people at our school think the AV Club is a bunch of geniuses, but it was a boneheaded move to believe that we could run into the library and expect to find a way out. We all knew that Mrs. Shh had long ago barricaded the back doors with bookshelves so she would be protected from things like air raids and junior prom season.

The four of us froze and stared at the impenetrable wall of bookshelves. There was no way we were getting out through the back.

Nerf and his pile of friends stormed in through the doors Mindy had knocked down earlier, and they stopped a few feet behind us. I could hear Mindy breathing hard while Xen, Owen, and I were breathing even harder.

None of us wanted to turn around and face the music, but we were trapped and had no other choice.

CHAPTER THREE

Lamer

"Now, what do we have here?" Nerf asked in a weird-sounding voice.

We turned around and what we saw almost caused us to fall over.

For some strange reason, Nerf and his friends looked like they were dressed up as LAME!

We all knew that Nerf admired our supergroup. Ever since he had witnessed us taking down the Fanatics two months ago, he has been a huge fan. He's worn homemade LAME T-shirts and drew our logo on the school walls. Nerf has talked nonstop about what amazing superheroes we are. He repeats any story he hears about us to everyone. Of course, he doesn't know we're LAME. If he did, there's no way he would want any part of it. But here he was with Mud, Weasel, and Mud's new girlfriend, Millie, doing some sort of cosplay and dressed up as us.

I glanced at my friends. They looked more confused than I was.

"Who are you?" I asked Nerf.

"We are your worst nightmares," he replied.

Owen panicked. "You're a small space that I have to share with a *pinching* clown?"

"They're not your literal nightmares," Mindy whispered.

"Splimpt," Owen said, using his favorite word. "That's a relief."

"Quiet," Nerf ordered. "Don't you recognize us? We are LAME."

"More like LAMER," Mindy mumbled.

"What did you say?" Mud asked angrily.

"Hey," Xen said bravely, "we're not looking for trouble."

"Really?" Weasel said. "Then what are you doing?"

"We were just running to the library to get a book," Xen lied.

"Right," Nerf said with a laugh. "People don't like books. You broke the office door, you broke the library doors, and now we're gonna broke your faces."

Don't you mean break our faces?

"Yeah," Mud's girlfriend, Millie, said. "Break your faces."

I wanted to use our powers, but if we did, our secret identities would be exposed, and our lives would be messier than they currently were. It looked like I was going to have to just stand there and get my face broken.

"You could just let us go," Xen suggested. "There's a one hundred percent chance we'd be grateful."

"That's okay," Nerf said. "I don't think Darth Susan would like us to do that."

Nerf jumped forward and tackled me. I fell against the edge of a book pit that Mrs. Shh had dug to imprison students with overdue book fines. I could hear my friends fighting Mud, Weasel, and Millie. Nerf gave me a knuckle sandwich right in the breadbasket. Normally I would love a sandwich, but this one made my stomach upset. I scrambled to stand up, and Nerf grabbed me by the wrist to keep me from running away. I saw Mindy standing next to me and being held in place by Millie. I turned my head as far as I could to the right and saw that Xen and Owen were also on their feet and being held captive by Mud and Weasel.

Nerf said a few mean things before they marched us to the gym bathroom. There, they used zombie-strength duct tape to stick us to the wall.

Mud looked confused, bewildered, stumped, and baffled all at once.

The four of them laughed for a few moments, and then Nerf took out a can of spray paint and climbed up me and Xen to paint something on the wall above us. They left the bathroom, laughing it up while putting us down.

We hung there on the bathroom wall, desperately trying to get ourselves off. I turned on the hand dryers and lights a couple of hundred times, but that didn't help. Owen tried to listen us free. That too failed. Mindy took Owen's suggestion and attempted to snap us loose. Every time she snapped, the tape stayed put while other bits of the bathroom and ceiling fell apart. After getting hit on the head by ceiling tiles a dozen times, she gave up. I think Xen tried to burp his way out of the tape, but he might have just been nervous.

An hour or so later, Tyler, the school janitor, came into the bathroom and found us hanging there.

I thought you four were supposed to be smart. Looks like I was wrong.

Tyler ripped some pieces of tape free, and we fell to the ground in an embarrassed heap of Geek. He looked around at the spray-painted wall and all the things that Mindy had broken with her clapping.

How about you stay around and help me clean up this bathroom?

We thanked him and then took off out of the bathroom and through the security hole. It was completely dark outside now, and Owen could hear a group of Fanatics roaming around two streets to the west and three streets south.

"This bites," Owen complained as we all stood there rubbing our tape burns.

"What is Darth Susan up to?" Mindy said, growling. "Is it her idea to have Nerf and his Neanderthals acting like LAME?"

"I still think her cruel-planner could have some answers," Xen insisted. "But it's not in her office."

"No," Xen whispered. "Not her house."

I nodded solemnly.

"This is madness," Owen hissed. "No one's ever gone to her house and lived to tell about it."

"That's not true," I argued. "No one's ever tried."

"Splimpt. Do we have to be the first?"

"No," I said. "But LAME does."

Mindy was right about the tagline. Without saying another word, the four of us slipped behind an abandoned RV that was parked in the middle of the street and went from Geek to LAME by changing into our outfits.

We had no time to lose!

CHAPTER FOUR

Honk Loudly

None of us had ever been to Darth Susan's house, mainly because none of us had ever wanted to go. But we knew where she lived, because she was constantly bragging about it.

How kind of me. You'd think that someone who lives at 1616 Faded Luster Way, in the Aspen Breeze Electric-Gated Neighborhood, shouldn't even have to bother with kids like you.

Darth Susan loved acting like she was better than others. Which was silly, seeing how the world was falling apart just as much for her as it was for everyone else. Her housing development was called the Aspen Breeze Electric-Gated Neighborhood. It had a ten-foot-tall electric fence around it, but there were tons of holes in the fence. The holes allowed the Fanatics to get in without any problem. Also, Darth Susan's neighborhood was near the government imitation-dairy factory, which meant that at any point during the day or night, there were Half-Deads walking through her streets in a dazed and tired state as they headed home from their jobs.

I had never wanted to visit Darth Susan. In fact I would be happy to never know anything personal about her. But if we wanted to be the kind of semi-superhero group that could be taken seriously, we needed to find out what she was up to. Superheroes don't get to pick the jobs they want.

I'd love to be like Dindo the elf king from the *Elf Scrimmage* game and spend my afternoons rescuing delinquent trolls from the Hall of Cake and Frosting.

But I wasn't like Dindo. I was a member of LAME, and because of that I had a confusing and odd duty to protect uncool stuff, like my school.

The four of us stayed in the shadows and worked our way quickly to Darth Susan's house. Owen kept his ears open and helped us avoid government curfew drones. He also kept an ear open for any Fanatics who were tearing things up, or trashing people, or mocking what they saw online.

When we got to the gate at the entrance to the Aspen Breeze Electric-Gated Neighborhood, we kept walking along the fence line until we found a hole we could slip through. Electricity runs through the wire, so we had to be careful not to come in contact with any of the metal.

"I never thought I'd be risking my life to visit Darth Susan," Owen said loudly as we carefully slipped through.

"Shhhhh," Mindy insisted.

"I hope we're not actually risking our lives," Xen complained. "We're just doing some sleuthing, right?"

"Danger sleuthing," I pointed out.

Once we were all through the fence, we crept behind a row of burnt trees. Even though Darth Susan's neighborhood was an electric-gated community, it was a lot like everywhere else in Piggsburg. Most of the houses had heavy security doors and windows and makeshift fences around torn-up lawns. Some had extra fences, and some were damaged from falling drones or Fanatics who had picked the yards apart. Most of the owners had stopped caring if their places looked nice.

"Can you hear anything?" I asked Owen.

He turned his head slowly, listening for any trace of Darth Susan's voice. His eyes lit up softly as he spoke.

"I can hear two people in that house over there." He pointed to a big house with a tall wooden fence around it. "They're arguing about who gets the last cup of powdered wheat milk. I can also hear a bunch of Half-Deads one street over making their way home. I don't hear any Fanatics, and no noise from Darth—wait, I got her." Owen's eyes went dark. "She's in her house, talking to Becky."

Mindy shivered. "I hate that lizard."

A Half-Dead dairy worker walked through one of the nearby holes in the fence. His shoulder bumped the fence, and a jolt of electricity shocked him into momentarily looking more than half dead.

"Maybe we should get out of here," Owen said. "Darth Susan isn't saying anything important, and it's not like we can just bust into her house and look at her planner."

"We're not going to," I reminded him. "LAME is."

"But that's us," Owen reminded me.

"I know, but if the world doesn't have LAME to fight its battles, who does it have? If children have no one to believe in, then what do they have? If a single person goes to bed tonight feeling hopeless, have we not failed?"

"We fail all the time," Xen reminded me.

"And lots of people go to bed hopeless," Mindy pointed out. "Have you looked around lately?"

"Fine," I said, bothered. "Maybe we're not much, but let's at least go to her house and see what we can find out."

"Okay," Mindy agreed. "But if she's talking baby talk to her lizard, I'm out."

As we made our way to Darth Susan's house, we passed two Half-Deads who were so tired they didn't recognize the four superheroes walking right by them. I'm not going to lie—it would have been nice to be noticed.

Yes, some people in Piggsburg were aware of us. Just

last week we put out a fire at the high school. The fire had started when the Science Clique got into a magnifying glass war with the Optics. Even my dad had heard about us from a couple of his co-workers. They had told him there were some superheroes in town who had fantastical powers.

Real-life fantastical powers! Blow-your-mind kind of stuff.

I didn't have the heart to inform my dad that the fantastical powers involved clapping and burping and me.

So we had a rising reputation, but tonight probably wouldn't change things, because there was no one other than uninterested Half-Deads to witness what we were doing.

When we got to 1616 Faded Luster Way, we stood under a dead tree and stared at the evil lair. Darth Susan's house was small, and the windows had bars over them. Her yard was rock and gravel, with thick green weeds growing everywhere. The front door was wooden and had a metal doorknob that looked as big as my head. Only two of her windows were lit up; otherwise the whole place was dark and foreboding.

"Is she saying anything now?" I whispered to Owen.

"What?"

I repeated myself a little louder.

She's scolding Becky for leaving lizard skin all over the floor.

"This is ridiculous," Mindy whispered loudly. "If we do get inside, how do we even know her planner's there? And if we find the planner, who knows if she wrote anything revealing."

A pack of Half-Deads shuffled across Darth Susan's front yard and down the street.

"Well, we won't know until we find out." I was being stubborn. "So, here's the plan: I'll start her car and get the horn honking. When she hears it, she'll come out to investigate. Xen and I will slip into her house and try to find the planner. You and Owen stay here, and if she decides to head back inside, break one of the windows to warn us."

Due to falling satellites, misguided drones, and screaming Fanatics, most buildings in Piggsburg don't have glass in their windows. It also doesn't help that many are busted by stray rocks that people throw when they're bored.

Amazingly, Darth Susan's house still had a few windows with glass. If necessary, Mindy could break one to warn us.

"Um . . ." Mindy said. "It's not much of a plan."

"And what about Becky?" Owen asked. "That lizard could be trouble."

"I have lizard repellent," Xen exclaimed. "I made it last week out of some things I found in my dad's junk drawer."

Xen pulled out a small jar that had holes in the lid. He shook some blue dust around our ankles and legs.

"We're good," he reported.

I didn't feel any better, but I didn't want to hurt Xen's feelings.

So, still hiding behind the dead tree, I thought of Darth Susan's car starting up and it did. I thought of the horn turning on and it happened. The noise was loud. In no time at all, the front door opened. Darth Susan stepped out, waving a flyswatter for protection. She had curlers in her hair and green lotion on her face, and she was wearing a robe made out of old towels.

Cover your butt—
you're about to
get swat!

Nobody answered her, and the car horn continued to sound.

"If you're messing with my vehicle, you'll pay dearly!" she warned.

No answer. More horn.

Darth Susan stepped all the way out and stomped through her rocky yard and toward the driveway. She was saying words that could easily get her into trouble. These days the government has drones that fly around listening for people who say words that the law thinks are offensive. Sometimes the drones will zap you, or they'll take your picture so that the government can bring you in to defend your vocabulary. Of course, people with money just pay the government a fee, and they get permission to say anything they want. Obviously, Darth Susan had paid someone, because she was using the kind of words no educator should.

As soon as she reached her car, Xen and I slipped out from behind the trees and moved up to the house. We ran across the porch and went in through the front door without being noticed.

I had hoped the planner would be lying out in the open, on a table or couch, but I couldn't see it anywhere. We dashed around the space carefully.

"What if it's in her room?" Xen asked, sounding worried.

We both looked toward a door on the right, off the kitchen. A board hanging on the door read . . .

THE QUEEN'S
CHAMBERS

Neither one of us wanted to see Darth Susan's bedroom. It was one thing to snoop around her house, but it felt much worse to go into her private quarters.

"We have no choice," Xen said.

He was right. We had gotten this far, and now, for the sake of all man, woman, and zombie kind, we had to look.

The car horn was still honking, so we knew that Darth Susan hadn't found a way to shut it off yet.

I nodded at Xen.

He gulped and then nodded at me.

Sometimes average superheroes have to do average things they don't want to do.

CHAPTER FIVE

Caught in the Act

We pushed open Darth Susan's bedroom door and carefully walked in. There were a couple of lit candles on a shelf. I was surprised to see that she had a bed. I had always pictured her sleeping on a nest made from old grocery bags. Her lizard-child, Becky, was sleeping on a big pillow in the corner and didn't seem to care that we had walked in.

"It's the lizard repellent," Xen whispered.

On the bedroom wall, there was a picture of Darth Susan and her pet:

Xen gagged. "That's not right."

"There's not much that's right with the world these days," I said. "Now look for . . . there it is!"

I pointed to a small desk in the corner. Sitting on top of the desk was the black cruel-planner. Stepping closer, I carefully opened the planner. Most of the dates were blank and cruelty-free, but when I flipped to the page from last Tuesday . . .

TUESDAY | WEDNESDAY

Meeting with Pep Liaison.

Meeting went well. The plan is a go.

"Hate is great." —Dufus

LAME

"What does it mean?" Xen asked. "And why did she write and circle *LAME* in the corner?"

Before I could answer, the car horn outside stopped honking.

"Oh no," Xen whispered.

We dashed out of the bedroom and into the kitchen. We were opening the back door and looking to break out, when we heard: "Hold on there!"

Xen and I froze.

We should have dashed out, but we were trained to be scared of Darth Susan, and now as she barked out a command, we stopped without thinking.

Freeze if you please! Actually, freeze if you don't please.

Xen and I turned around slowly and locked eyes with her. Whispering, I said to Xen . . .

"What do you think you're doing?" she asked loudly. "And stop whispering."

I opened my mouth to answer her, but before I could say anything, she threw out a few more words of her own.

She stopped for a second to wag her finger at us. Then she continued.

"I need people to believe that you are the real LAME," Darth Susan growled. "Why did you come here? Is there an emergency of some sort?"

We both shook our heads.

"Then let's get you out."

She pushed us through the back door and onto a small porch that was surrounded by barbed wire. She stepped out with us and shut the door behind her. I saw some Half-Deads in the distance, and the air was filled with the sound of dogs howling.

"Don't ever come to my house again," she warned. "I'm having you do this for one reason only. And you visiting me isn't the reason."

I had no idea what she was talking about. Darth Susan was acting like we were supposed to understand what was going on.

"Are those your costumes, then?" she asked.

We nodded.

"Not bad. I've never seen those real troublemakers,

but you look LAME to me. Did anyone see you tonight, Nerf?"

I tried not to appear shocked. Darth Susan thought I was Nerf dressed up as LAME! Me and Nerf didn't look anything alike, but apparently the costume was fooling her.

"Did they see you?" she asked again.

I shook my head.

"That's not good. We need people to see what you look like, so he'll believe me. Why do you think I told the students to take pictures of you?"

"But . . ." Xen started to say something. I elbowed him to shut up.

"Where are the other two?" she asked.

I tried to imitate Nerf's LAME voice. "We're going to get them now."

Darth Susan stared at me. "Are you okay?" she asked impatiently.

"Fine," I said in my Nerfiest voice.

"Get going," she insisted. "Try to act heroic, and remember: I'm going to need you to show up at the theaters tomorrow night to meet him."

"At the theaters?" I Nerfed.

"Yes, at the theaters. And you need to drink something," she complained. "It sounds like you're getting sick."

I did a small fake cough.

"Go."

Darth Susan made a noise that let us know she was disgusted with us. She turned around and went back into her house. Xen and I just stood there in shock. A moaning Half-Dead shuffled by us to the right.

I hate this neighborhood.

Yeah, the curb appeal is awful.

The two of us stepped off the porch and out the barbed-wire gate. We slipped around the side of the house and returned to the row of burnt bushes.

Mindy and Owen were waiting there for us.

"Thanks for coming to our rescue," Xen said sarcastically.

"We knew you were okay," Mindy replied defensively. "Owen could hear everything. I can't believe she thought you were Nerf. And what plan is she talking about?"

"I don't know," I answered. "But for some reason, she has Nerf and his friends dressing up to get their pictures taken by Fanatics. And they're going to be at the theaters tomorrow to meet someone."

All four of us were silent for a few moments as we pondered what this could mean. Eventually, Owen broke the silence.

"Splimpt. I can hear Fanatics two streets over."

That was our cue to leave the Aspen Breeze Electric-Gated Neighborhood and make our way back to our houses.

I had no trouble getting home. Unless you consider a government drone shining its light on me trouble.

In this day and age, bossy drones aren't a huge worry. They're just another normal occurrence we have to deal with. They're always shouting things at everyone.

The drone followed me for a bit, making fun of how I ran. So I did some more funny running and headed down an alley and through a tunnel to lose it and make my way home.

CHAPTER SIX
Something's Wrong

I woke up the next morning and foraged for something edible to eat in my backyard. I found a couple of breakfast bacon weeds and two egg-shaped wild carrots.

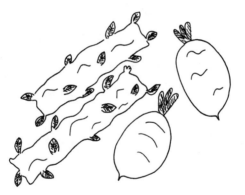

There was a little bit of food in the house, but I was tired of eating stale marshmallows and dehydrated crickets. Grocery shopping had been extra bad lately. My mom was coming home with stuff much grosser than usual.

It was a new day, but my mind was still preoccupied with what had happened the night before. I wanted to know why Darth Susan was working with Nerf. It made me mad to think she was using LAMER to do her bidding. People didn't know that wasn't us. What if LAMER did something awful and turned the world against us? We'd have to go into hiding for the rest of our days.

After eating my breakfast, I took a twenty-second government-sanctioned cold shower. Then I got dressed and headed to WADD. Owen met up with me as I was leaving my front yard.

"I heard you getting ready," he informed me. "So I knew you'd be coming out now."

"You listen to me getting ready?"

"Yes, and I heard everything. Those dehydrated crickets really work a number on your digestive system."

It was not comforting to know that Owen could hear private things so well.

When we got to WADD, we were both surprised to see four NPs standing in front of the security hole. There were two more standing by the flagpole. NPs are troopers for the government's private army. They were recently sponsored by a ginormous company called NinCon, a conglomerate of nine companies that sell air and water to countries that need it. And since the whole world needs those things, NinCon is a very rich and powerful business—rich enough to sponsor an army.

At first everyone called the troopers NTs because saying "NinCon Troopers" was too much of a mouthful. But the people who thought the NinCon Troopers were obnoxious began calling them NinCon Poopers, or NPs, behind their backs.

NinCon Pooper reporting for duty.

You probably shouldn't say "duty," Mr. Pooper.

Owen and I crouched behind a cement wall near the front of the school. The wall was half destroyed, but it provided a good place to hide and view the area.

"Why are there NPs here?" he asked.

"Maybe they've come for us," Mindy said.

We turned around and saw Mindy.

"Why would they want us?" I questioned.

"What's happening?" Xen said as he arrived at the broken wall and knelt down next to Mindy. "Is this a meeting I wasn't invited to? Because I've calculated the odds, and I'd be ninety-seven percent offended."

"No," Owen told him. "There are NinCon Poopers in front of the school."

The four of us then watched as a steady stream of students went through the hole. The NPs just stood there looking stiff and aloof.

"Maybe they're here to help us feel safe," Xen suggested.

We all laughed.

The government rarely wants us to feel safe. They just want us to go to work, go to school, and stay in our houses without causing them trouble.

Xen nervously burped.

"Well," Mindy said with resolve, "we won't find out why they're here from here."

She stood up and stepped out from behind the wall. The rest of us did the same. Holding our heads up high and trying to look brave, we walked across the street, toward the front of the school. I looked around for something I could turn on or off with my ability if a fight broke out. But there was nothing for me to turn on, and no reason to worry, because the NPs didn't even glance at us as we walked past them and slipped through the hole.

Inside the school, I saw two more NPs down the hall and three walking into the office. All the students were talking loudly and discussing the fact that our school had too much authority on hand today. I spotted a couple of Sox who weren't sliding and a Goth who was trying hard to look uninterested in everything.

When I got to my first-hour class, Mr. Upwonder wasn't there yet, and an NP was standing at the front of the class-room. Everyone was sitting quietly in their seats. The NPs were not people to mess with. They kept the peace for the government by roughing people up and taking away what little freedom we still had.

From two desks over, Owen coughed, and one of the NPs stared at him like he had just beaten up a high-ranking government official. Owen slid down in his seat.

Finn the crier cried out.

Ten minutes after the first announcement, the classroom door opened, and Mr. Upwonder came in. His face was pale, and he looked emotionally and physically confused. He nodded at the NP and then sat down behind his desk at the front of the room. Mr. Upwonder was one of the nicer Staffers. He at least tried to get along with the students at WADD. Lots of times he would begin class with a joke.

The intercom crackled to life and everyone jumped. The crackling was followed by Darth Susan's horrible voice.

Good morning, wonderful WADDs.

As usual, she was way off. Nothing about this morning felt good.

"As your simple faces can see," she continued, "there are NinCon Troopers here at the school today. In a few moments, they will begin escorting classes to the auditorium, where there will be a mandatory announcement. Obey all orders they give you, and be quietly grateful that your government has such a strong concern for your well-being. That is all."

The speaker snapped off.

Our room was silent again. The NP at the front looked at all of us and sniffed aggressively. It didn't make me feel grateful in the least.

"Stand," he ordered.

Everyone obeyed, even Mr. Upwonder.

"Follow me," the NP barked. "Staffers in the rear."

After forming a single line, the entire class followed the NP out of the room. In the hall, other classes were following their NPs and quietly moving toward the auditorium. My stomach was not enjoying this. Not only did it feel like we were marching toward something horrible, but the breakfast weeds I had eaten were not agreeing with me. I wanted to dash off and escape, but I'm not sure my abilities were a match for the small legion of NinCon Poopers here today.

We reached the assembly hall and were directed into our seats. I sat next to Owen. Mindy was one row in front of us, while Xen was one row back. I could see Nerf and his friends sitting together near the front row. They were dressed as themselves, not LAMER.

Up onstage there were four empty chairs and a podium with a microphone. Normally, setting up the microphone was the duty of the AV Club. But nothing was normal these days.

Once we were all seated, the NPs took their places at the end of each row, blocking us from getting up and leaving.

The auditorium doors were then closed and locked.

Middle school is hard. That's just a fact. I'm sure even in the olden days, it was difficult due to homework and hormones and bullies and grades and boredom. But these days it is even worse. With things like wicked weather, wicked government, and wicked Fanatics, life can get unbearable. Now we had been herded into the auditorium and were being held captive.

"I'm going to throw up," Owen whispered.

"Quiet!" the NP nearest us snapped.

Darth Susan walked onto the stage and took a seat in one of the four chairs. I spotted Principal Woth hiding behind two heavy curtains at the back of the stage.

A gaggle of NPs marched onto the stage and stood near the edge, looking out at the audience. They all had on their official yellow helmets and deathly serious expressions. A senior NP entered and walked up to the podium. He checked his watch three times, as if waiting for a certain time to arrive. I spotted Finn the crier—he was sitting in the front and not saying a word. I had never heard our school so quiet.

The senior NP stared at his watch for at least two more minutes before he finally looked up and spoke:

None of us felt good about what was happening.

"Once the announcement is made, you will all remain in your seats," the NP continued. "No standing, no moving, and no disorder. Any disobedience will be dealt with accordingly."

The senior NP removed a tablet from a leather bag and turned it on. He held the large tablet up to the microphone on the podium.

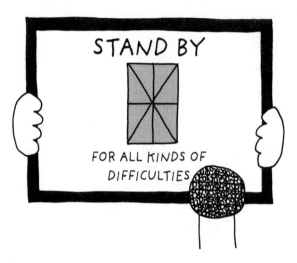

The tablet began to play the SUSDSA irrational anthem, the music piped through the microphone filling the room with added dread.

". . . what so proudly we cower under the Fanatic last screaming. And the selfies flash bright, there is little reason to fight. Just hide in your homes till you're told to hide elsewhere."

With the music playing, it was now obvious what was about to go down. We were going to be addressed by the president of the SUSDSA, President Flake. It had happened a few times in my life, and it was never good. It had never happened quite like this, though. Usually, drones would just shout things down at everyone.

The irrational anthem stopped playing, and President Flake's face appeared on the tablet screen.

CHAPTER SEVEN

The Announcement

> My fellow Somewhat United, Sort of Divided people of the States of America. It is my great pleasure to greet you this morning. As you know, I have dedicated my life to making you all safe and comfortable.

I wanted to roll my eyes, but I knew that the government was working on anti-eyerolling technology, and I didn't want to risk being caught.

Thanks to me, we are much better off now than we were last year. I actually have two more homes and three new cars. So, that proves that things are better for everyone.

I looked around, wondering who was hoarding all the peace and prosperity. My life certainly didn't have an excess of it. I was also curious if anyone was buying what Flake was selling. No disrespect to the president, but everyone knew he was awful. He was only the president because the one before him had given up when the job got too hard. Flake never seemed to do anything to help anybody. He just stayed in the Blight House, making dumb laws and sending out drones to enforce them.

Today I bring you the biggest announcement I've ever announced!

My carrot-and-bacon-weeds-filled stomach tightened with fear.

"After much complicated and secret negotiation," he continued, "and with some clandestine activity, I am finally pleased to announce that your government has come to an agreement with the Fanatics."

Everyone gasped.

"It required great effort, but we have done it. We have made a fourth Sand Throwers movie, based on the fourth book, *Gritty*."

My heart stopped beating.

I couldn't believe it. I would have been less surprised if the king of New Kansas had stopped in and given us all corn tanks. There was going to be a fourth movie? The terrible third movie was one of the main reasons the world had become so messed up.

The place erupted in cheers and excitement.

It took a load of loud, threatening orders from the NPs to get things quieted down. President Flake had kept silent, letting the news sink in all over the world, but now he was talking again.

The project has been kept under tight wraps. But it is my pleasure to inform you that the movie will be screened worldwide in just two days. Tickets go on sale tomorrow. Mention this announcement and receive two percent off. Just pay a two percent service fee.

There was more chaos. The NPs pulled out their fear horns and blew until we were all forced to plug our ears.

President Flake continued. "We recognize that one of the few problems we have not been able to solve is the Fanatics. So, in a historic attempt at achieving peace, we are reaching out to them. A treaty has been signed, and it was agreed that in exchange for a well-made fourth movie, they will stop their reign of annoying terror. This movie has everything they've ever wanted: excitement, cuter actors, better dialogue, and a satisfying conclusion to Ky-Ryder's emotional problems. It will help usher in a new decade of peace and stability for the entire planet."

I glanced around.

Everybody looked excited—even the Goths were smiling. The only people who appeared nervous were me and my friends. There had to be a connection to what Darth Susan was up to and the release of the fourth movie.

Flake talked on. "There will be major punishments for anyone who seeks to disrupt things or spread chaos as we prepare for the movie's release. The film will not be shown if the peace treaty is broken in any way. Your local officials will issue further instructions as needed. So stay calm and remember: If you don't, we'll make you."

The screen with Flake's image flashed once and then went dark.

Everybody wanted to discuss what the president had

said, but we weren't allowed to. The NPs ordered all of us to stand up. We were then ushered back to our classrooms.

Sadly, the NPs didn't leave. They stayed at our school to make sure that everything remained oppressive. I couldn't talk to my friends or go to the Geek Cave, because there were way too many eyes watching. At lunch the NPs' stares made everyone uneasy.

My last class was Apocalyptic Economics 101, and our teacher, Ms. Fitz, read us the official peace treaty that President Flake and the leader of the Fanatics had signed. The document basically said that all Fanatics would behave if the government's movie made up for the faults of the third one in the series.

After reading the treaty, Ms. Fitz went into the boring economics of our time.

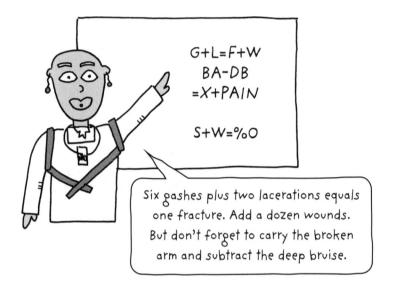

$G+L=F+W$
$BA-DB$
$=X+PAIN$

$S+W=\%O$

Six gashes plus two lacerations equals one fracture. Add a dozen wounds. But don't forget to carry the broken arm and subtract the deep bruise.

I didn't care what gash plus laceration equaled. I only cared about the time. I needed the school day to end so that LAME could gather and discuss our course of action. But instead I was stuck learning about how to properly add painful things and how to invest in spears and wheat.

Ten minutes before class was over, the speaker on the wall crackled and hummed to life. Darth Susan's Vader voice filled the room.

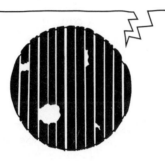

Attention: This has been a historic day. Earth will never be the same. The fourth movie, *Gritty*, arrives in two days. By law, anyone who agrees to wait respectfully will be allowed to start lining up in the nearest theater compound. And due to my large heart, those of you here at Otto Waddle who feel the need to wait in line early are free to leave now. That is all.

Ms. Fitz and a handful of students got up and left the classroom. The movie wasn't going to show for two days, but the madness was already beginning.

I knew that the Fanatics had reached an agreement with the government, but what if the movie turned out bad? What if it was worse than the third one? I'm just not sure me and my friends could survive the aftermath of another bad movie.

LAME couldn't meet in the Geek Cave after school

because the NPs escorted everyone off campus and ordered us all to get home immediately.

The four of us walked together and worried aloud about what was happening.

"Is this a good thing?" Xen asked. "I mean, maybe the movie will bring peace. Of course, I've calculated the odds, and they aren't good."

Owen had something to say:

I'm just excited to see how they resolve Ky-Ryder's story.

We all stopped walking to stare at him.

"What?" Owen said defensively. "My parents made me watch the third movie. If it helps, I didn't enjoy most of it."

Mindy shook her head. "That's just sad."

Mindy hates the Sand Thrower series more than anyone else I know. She hates that it appealed to so many people who she thinks are shallow and awful. The kind of people who have helped tear our world apart. Also, it bothers her that everyone assumes that she loves the books and movies simply because she's a girl who likes to read.

I bet you just love these books.

I bet you're wrong.

"A fourth movie is only going to make things worse," she told us. "The Fanatics will find something to hate about it, and that will be the end of civilization."

"So, do we still care about Darth Susan?" I questioned.

"I never really cared about her in the first place," Owen admitted.

"Right," I replied. "But do we care about what she might be up to? She must have known about the movie announcement before anyone else did. How? She might be powerful at WADD, but the government's not going to give her that kind of information. Why did she form a fake LAME?"

"All of that matters," Owen said. "So we should go to the theater compound immediately. Then we can stake out a place in line and vigilantly guard the city and figure out things from there."

I'm not watching the movie, and I'm certainly not waiting in line like a bunch of dumb sheep with bad taste in movies. I've got better things to do!

"Like what?" Xen asked.

Mindy frowned. "I don't know, anything. Breathing. Sleeping. Anything."

Owen sighed. "Fine. It's just that the theater compound seems like a good place to keep an eye on things. Darth Susan said she'd be there with LAMER, and she also said that we're allowed to wait in line. That's pretty generous. Do you think the fourth movie is already beginning to soften her up? If the announcement can make her nicer, then maybe the movie will change the world for good."

"Has the government ever done anything good for anyone?" I asked.

"They handed out cups and bandages at that last Piggsburg city fear-a-thon," Owen reminded us.

"Yeah," I said with disgust. "But the cups were empty when the runners needed water. They were just a shameless promotional item for the government."

"And the bandages they gave out were used," Xen said.

"Besides," I reminded them, "this isn't *just* about the government or the movie. This is about LAMER. We have to put an end to impostors trying to steal our identity!"

"I don't know," Owen said. "It's kind of flattering to have my identity stolen. It's probably the first time anyone's wanted to imitate me. Well, unless you count all the times people have done mean impressions."

I'm Owen, and my hair looks like a big bird poop, and I probably pick my nose.

"Nerf, Mud, Weasel, and Millie are bullies," I reminded them. "And if we let this go, they might turn into super-bullies."

"I hate to say it, but maybe Owen's right," Mindy admitted. "The movie line might be the best spot for gathering information tonight."

"Okay," I said. "Can all of you sneak out of your houses later tonight without your parents noticing?"

Easy. There's a large hole in our kitchen where a drone crashed through.

My parents lock themselves in their panic room at six. They won't notice I'm gone.

My parents are away at SadCon. General Freeloader from the General Freeloader series is going to be there in person.

"Good," I said. "Then let's meet at Owen's house. Also, we should wear our night outfits."

Everyone was on board with that suggestion, largely because we liked wearing our night outfits. They were basically the same as our day ones, but all black. Xen insisted his had flames on the side, but since they were also black, you couldn't see them.

A drone above us began to bark orders for everyone on the streets to move along. We split up and made our way to our disheveled, unstable homes.

Move it or lose it! Wait, you've got nothing to lose, so just move it!

CHAPTER EIGHT

Spotted and Spoiled

My parents, like the rest of the world, were jazzed about the fourth movie. My dad's work had shut down for the day because of the announcement. Most of the planet was hopeful that this dumb movie would help fix all our problems.

If it's good, there will be peace on Earth.

If it's bad, there will be pieces on Earth of everything, including us.

If the movie was bad, the Fanatics would freak, but I have to admit it was nice to see my parents pumped about something. Normally they just spent time complaining about the weird weather we always had and their jobs.

My dad worked for the government, driving a supply truck. It's a pretty dangerous job, but only because he's a horrible driver. He runs into about ten things a day. My mom hates receiving his texts.

> I ran over an abandoned watchtower today. It almost crushed me.

> That's not funny!

> Okay, how about knock, knock.

> Who's there?

> Not my front bumper or windshield. They were destroyed by the falling tower.

I guess it's lucky that the truck my dad drives is big and banged up. Because of that he rarely gets hurt, and his boss never notices when there are new dents or missing bumpers.

My mom's job is less collision-filled. She spends her day foraging for food at the grocery store and collecting rocks to recycle at the gravel factory. She also volunteers at the local powdered-soup kitchen. They're good parents, but I wish I had a brother or sister so that it wasn't always just me and them.

After eating dinner, I put on a first-rate act of pretending to be tired and going to bed. When the house was quiet, I slipped out the back door, through the broken fence in the yard, and around the house to Oak Street.

I never enjoy being out on the streets at night. Lately the government has been using drones to take pictures of people breaking curfew. They like to use those photos to harass people.

#CaughtWhereIShouldntBe
#DontLookAtMe
#DownWithDrones

The Fanatics don't mind the pictures—they just post them online. It's one of the reasons why the government can't control them. While everyone stays hunkered down in their homes at night, the Fanatics roam freely, complaining about the third movie and ambushing people with unwanted makeovers.

To avoid all of that, we try to stay in the shadows, or blend in with a pack of wild dogs, or dress in dark clothing like nerdy ninjas.

Now I was dressed in black and moving easily through the streets on my way to Owen's. Only a few stray dogs payed any attention to me. I really did feel better knowing that thanks to their agreement with the government, there were no Fanatics outside. I got all the way to Owen's house without being subjected to an abusive selfie. Which was kind of a crime, seeing how cool I looked in my night outfit.

Out of all the AV Club members' houses, Owen's was in the worst shape. It was in a part of town where Fanatics and Half-Deads loved to trample and mess up everything. Owen's dad, Mr. Glip, doesn't pick up their yard, plus he collects trash and keeps it all over their house. He loves his garbage and hates when we come over, because he thinks we're going to take something.

Don't touch any of my treasures. Hands off my booty.

So we don't hang out at Owen's house very much. But since his parents were off at SadCon, it was a perfect place to make plans.

As darkness settled over Piggsburg, Owen filled us in on what he could hear happening.

"The theaters in the theater compound already have huge lines," he reported. "The government has set up a bunch of tents, and the crowds are getting bigger by the minute."

"This movie better be good," Xen said nervously.

Films really aren't the same as they used to be. Since the third Sand Thrower flick and the ensuing Theater Wars, the government had gone to war against privately owned theaters. The theaters tried to fight back, but the government was too powerful.

The privately owned theaters were forced to close, and the government constructed massive theater compounds in most towns. The compounds were like small cities with a lot of ugly square buildings surrounded by big cinder-block walls. Now the government films and shows the movies it wants while controlling who sees what, and when they see them.

Owen was shaking. "There's probably a few hundred people already waiting in line."

"Is it me," I asked, "or are people losing their minds?"

"It's a little of both," Mindy replied.

As usual, she was right.

CHAPTER NINE

Hard to Imitate

"Wait!" Owen lifted his ear to the wind. "I can hear Darth Susan. She's there talking to some students in line."

"Why?" I asked.

"I'm not sure what's happening," Owen admitted, "but she's telling a Goth that she's proud of him for waiting."

"We need to get over there and do some snooping," I said.

I do like snooping!

We traveled as shadowy ninjas through the streets, with Owen keeping his ears open. The Piggsburg theater compound was a few miles away from Owen's house. Not to tear down LAME, but we all were more winded than a real superhero group probably should be after going on a walk.

The compound was on the south end of town, near the corporate gravel and gruel factory.

The theaters were ugly. Plus, the government designed the seats to be hard and scratchy, making it difficult for people to stay seated for long. My dad claims they did that so moviegoers have to get up and walk around the lobby. That way the government can sell them more high-priced and highly horrible theater snacks.

When we got to the compound, I was impressed by the size of the crowd. I was also impressed by how calm everyone was acting. There were hordes of people beneath tents that the government had set up to provide temporary protection from the elements.

All the sections and parts of the line were numbered and divided up. There were also rows and rows of government-sponsored toilets and NPs everywhere.

But it didn't look like the NPs were even needed. Everyone seemed to be behaving themselves just fine. They were all standing in a line beneath the tents and talking quietly. Ms. Fitz had told us earlier that the peace treaty said,

Citizens are hereby allowed to wait in an organized manner at the theater compound nearest them. There shall be very little chitting and only small amounts of chatting.

Well, people were chitting and chatting at respectable volumes, and nobody was shouting or misbehaving. It was eerie to witness Fanatics acting civil while quietly posting pictures and taking snapshots.

#InLineAndInStyle
#WaitingIsTheHardestPart
#TheMovieBetterBeGood
#SelfieForTheSoul
#SoIntoMyself
#TeamKy-Ryder
#DuckFaceForTheHumanRace

Owen tapped me on the shoulder. "I can hear Darth Susan. She's over there."

Pretending to be shadows, we crept along the side of the wall.

"I can't believe that no one is fighting or screaming," Mindy said, dumbfounded.

"Supercreepy," I replied.

"I'm okay with it," Xen told us.

Just past the sixth theater, I saw Darth Susan talking to some Pens who were standing in line. Pens are a group of students at WADD who are always writing things. They're kind of annoying because they also like to talk about how great they are at writing and tell you everything about the current story they're working on.

So then the protagonist, who is an orphan, has to complete his hero's journey while simultaneously discovering a cure for the broken heart.

I just said hello.

The Pens are one of the less threatening cliques at our school. Most people think that the AV Club should get along with them. But me and my friends like things to be a bit more technical than pens and paper.

Mindy, Owen, Xen, and I snuck behind a dumpster to properly spy on Darth Susan. The dumpster was filled with a group of Fanatics who were softly singing about the Sand Thrower series. The song was awful, but our view of Darth Susan was worse. From where we stood she looked happy and smiley and . . . kind?

"What's going on?" I asked in a whispered panic.

Xen burped. "I don't know, but seeing her smile like that makes me nervous."

Darth Susan looked at her watch as she talked to the Pens and then smiled even bigger. She glanced up at the sky as if expecting to see something.

"Look!" Mindy whispered.

I peered over the dumpster. People in line were murmuring and talking louder. I also saw something much more irritating.

Standing on the road next to the thirty-fifth portion of the line were Nerf, Mud, Weasel, and Millie. They were in their costumes and walking like they thought they were all that and a tub of dip. The crowd thought they were the real

LAME that they had heard about. A few people began to clap and smile.

My blood boiled.

It was horrible that LAMER was pretending to be us. And what made it worse was that everyone seemed to . . .

Nerf raised his hands and declared to the crowd, "LAME has arrived."

People applauded respectfully as a few NPs stood by, monitoring the situation for volume and unruliness.

I was angry. It made me feel even worse that we were

stuck hiding behind a dumpster while Nerf was in front of everyone, getting praise that belonged to us. He spoke up, using his weird fake voice.

"Feel free to worship us," he told the crowd. "You have probably heard that we've been helping this town these last two months. But don't think of us as superheroes. Think of us as *your* superheroes. Piggsburg is a place that's better, thanks to us."

My ears began to steam.

Not everyone in town knows about us and LAME. But Nerf was acting like the entire world knew and worshipped them . . . I mean, us!

I growled softly. "He's going to ruin our small reputations."

"We have a reputation?" Owen asked sadly. "I've always wanted a rep."

"You've always had one," Mindy whispered. "It just wasn't good."

"I don't understand." For a person with such a high IQ, Xen was confused. "How can they pretend to be us? They don't have any powers."

Nerf held up his hands again.

People, we just want everyone to know that we are here to save things and do good stuff.

"And we would never use such bad grammar," Mindy said angrily.

I couldn't take what Nerf was doing any longer. So, I shouted loudly over the top of the dumpster.

"IF YOU REALLY ARE LAME, THEN SHOW US YOUR POWERS!"

A few people looked around, trying to see who had just yelled that.

"Yeah," one of the Pens in line said. "We want to see your powers."

"Um, well, the thing, the thing is . . ." Nerf stuttered.

Fly so I can finally have something good to post!

Nerf looked nervous and less confident. I liked where this was going.

"Please fly for us!" a Fanatic screamed.

Weasel held out his hands and motioned for the crowd to settle down.

Three NPs moved in closer.

The presence of LAMER was getting everyone riled up, and according to the peace treaty, riling things up was off limits.

People, we can't show you our powers because we are to humble.

Owen bristled. "I can hear that he used the wrong *to*."

I was impressed. Apparently, Owen's superhearing worked on grammar.

"At least make some fire with your fists!" someone yelled at Nerf.

"Or shoot lasers out of your eyes!"

"Yeah," an NP said while stepping closer to LAMER. "Shoot lasers out of your eyes."

The people didn't seem mad or angry. They just wanted to witness a display of superpowers.

"Again," Nerf insisted, "it's wrong to be a show-off."

"Show off! Show off! Show off!" the NPs and the crowd chanted loudly.

Millie growled at the gathering, but that only made them more excited.

"Show off! Show off!" everyone screamed.

Nerf was sweating. "I'm sorry," he yelled. "There isn't time for us to show off. We must go and help those who are less cool than we are."

Then, in a move that looked like they had practiced earlier, Nerf, Mud, Weasel, and Millie all simultaneously turned around and took off running.

The crowd clapped for the fleeing heroes as the NPs tried to calm things down.

"No fair," Xen said as we huddled back behind the dumpster. "I've always wanted people to clap for me."

"I don't get it." I was genuinely upset. "Why is Darth Susan having Nerf and his friends pretend to be us, and what is the connection to— Wait." We had been so caught up with LAMER that nobody noticed the disappearance of Darth Susan. "Where'd she go?"

"I didn't see," Xen said, beginning to get belchy.

"Can you hear her?" Mindy asked Owen.

Owen shook his head. "Wherever she went, she isn't talking."

"Then let's spread out and find her. She put LAMER

together, she knew about this movie, and she's up to some-thing that might ruin our lives. We'll split up, stick to the shadows, and text when one of us finds her."

I went east, Mindy went west, Owen went south, and, due to nervousness, Xen went to find a bathroom.

CHAPTER TEN

Stalking the 'Tary

It didn't take more than a few moments for me to realize how difficult finding Darth Susan was going to be. The crowd was too big, the night was too dark, and a pollution fog was rolling in and making things look fuzzy. Everyone began to put on their government-issued breathing masks that we were all required to carry.

I took off my LAME mask and put on my breather. The pollution-filled night made me question my life choices. Here I was at a gathering for a movie I didn't care about, surrounded by people I didn't want to be hanging around with, and looking for the secretary from my school who I didn't like.

I was planning to keep complaining in my head, but my eyes spotted something disgusting—lizard poop. Down on the ground there was a tiny trail of the white stuff I knew so well. I don't know what Darth Susan fed Becky, but for some reason the poop glowed under the moonlight. I was actually happy to see it, because where there was poop, there was Darth Susan.

I followed the glowing poop trail until I spotted her.

Darth Susan was slipping between a crowd of Fanatics standing in line and the outside wall of theater twelve. She glanced around to see if anyone was watching.

Then she moved on.

Carefully I ran to theater twelve and past the one hundred and seventh section of the line. I had to move fast not to lose her. On the other side of theater twelve, there were more tents, and more people, and more NPs. And in the distance, I saw the back of Darth Susan.

This was not the time to be working alone.

I took out my phone and texted Mindy while I followed Darth Susan. After hitting Send on my phone, I worked my way a little closer to our suspicious school secretary. She slipped down an alley between theaters fourteen and fifteen.

I slipped through after her.

The alley was long and emptied out into an open space at the rear of the theater compound. I could see a field that was covered with piles and piles of comfortable old movie seats the government had taken out. The rows of chairs were piled up and covered with dirt and weeds.

I took out my phone to text Owen and Xen, but there was a problem.

In an effort to protect you, your government has temporarily shut down all Wi-Fi and phones. That is all. Actually, that's not all. We will no longer provide government cheese.

"Cratch," I swore in Elf.

The government always delivers bad news in twos. That way when people get angry, they give us back one of the things and trick us into thinking we've won. My guess is that they ran out of cheese and knew that would tear us apart. So they took away our Wi-Fi for a moment. When they give us back the Wi-Fi, we'll be so happy that we won't complain about the cheese.

I wasn't too broken up about the cheese, because government cheese isn't easy to digest. It does things to your body that are embarrassing and uncomfortable.

Stepping between piles of old seats, I searched the dark field for Darth Susan. There was no more glowing poop. I needed Owen and his glowing eyes.

"Owen," I whispered into the dark, hoping that wherever he was, he could hear me. "It's Tip. I'm back behind theaters 14 and 15, and Darth Susan is here somewhere. It would be great if you guys could come quickly. Oh yeah, sorry about the cheese."

Owen loved government cheese, and I knew he'd be bummed about the bad dairy news.

I was about to sit down on one of the abandoned seats and wait for my friends, when in the distance, across many mounds of old chairs, I saw a small door open and a faint glow light up the area. I couldn't see what building the door was attached to, but I saw the silhouette of Darth Susan. She stepped inside, and the door shut.

Everything was black again.

"Come on, Tip," I said in an effort to psych myself up. "You can do this."

I crept across the field, moving cautiously through the dark. I tripped a couple of dozen times before reaching the building Darth Susan had entered. It was made of brick, and from what I could see, it was tall.

I rubbed my hands over the building and found the door.

Locked.

Normally a locked door would be a problem, but this door had an electronic lock. I thought of it being open, and there was a soft whirring noise followed by a crisp *click*. Taking two deep breaths, I attempted to calm my nerves.

"Owen," I whispered aloud. "Where are you guys?"

My hearing wasn't super, but I could imagine that wherever Owen was, he was probably crying about the cheese and not listening to me.

I pushed down the lever and opened the door just a little. Light spilled out from the opening like white glue, and I had to take a moment to let my eyes adjust.

Cautiously I stuck my head in the door. It was a large warehouse crammed with movie sets and props that the government used to make its propaganda movies. Some theater compounds around the world had secret studios, and apparently our theater was one of them. The government said the movies they made weren't political, but I don't think anyone believed that. Last year they released a movie called *Indiana Jones and the Importance of Obeying Your Leaders*. I hated it, but Xen thought it was okay.

I liked the part where the leaders gave everyone the chance to pay their taxes.

I pushed the door open some more and slunk inside. I took off my pollution mask and breathed in.

The warehouse smelled old and dusty.

I walked past a row of big roman columns and a fake mechanic's garage complete with fake cars and fake floors.

A set next to it was decorated like a castle, and there was a huge painting of palm trees that was as large as a wall.

After winding halfway through the stuffed warehouse, I finally heard someone talking and popped back behind a fake refrigerator in a fake kitchen near a fake bathroom.

"I promise you they're coming."

The voice belonged to Darth Susan. I couldn't see her from behind the fridge, but I could see the boy she was talking to.

I hope so, Aunt Susan. I'm making a huge sacrifice for you. So you'd better come through. Do you know how many people would kill for the information I gave you?

"Yes, Milton," Darth Susan said. "But only because you keep telling me that."

"Why did you want to know what day the movie was being released?" he asked her.

"Let's just say it's important to my retirement."

"I wasn't supposed to tell anyone," he rambled on. "Not a soul. Just like I'm not supposed to tell people that each theater around the world will be receiving their copies of the movie on a flash drive that will be delivered by drones. The one for this theater compound arrives at ten a.m. on the day of the movie."

"That's great," Darth Susan said. "I only needed to know what day."

"And I only need to meet up with your friends."

"Don't worry, they will show up. They do what—"

Darth Susan was interrupted by the sound of something stomping toward them from the opposite direction.

"Here they are now," she said smugly.

I couldn't see who was coming, but I saw the Milton kid getting excited.

"Yes!" he cheered. "Yes."

I tried to see what was happening, but from where I was, I had no real view.

"We've arrived!" a voice announced.

They were still out of view, but I knew it was Nerf and his friends—LAMER had arrived.

"Great dusty widgets!" Milton cheered.

"Miton," Darth Susan said, "this is LAME."

My face burned with anger and sicktitude. These lame impostors were like a dumb dream that wouldn't go away.

I needed to see more.

Quietly I dropped to my hands and knees and crawled across the fake kitchen to the fake bathroom. I crouched behind a big clawfoot bathtub and looked up over the rim. I could see everyone now—Darth Susan, Milton, and all the wannabe LAMEs.

"Thank you so much, LAME," Milton groveled. "First off, it's a pleasure to meet all of you. I've heard stories about you. And let me say, I am a big fan."

"Right," Milton agreed. "Well, I know it's a long shot, but I've always dreamed of playing a superhero in a movie, and my chances would be much better if I had some actual experience. So I was hoping—well, my aunt said maybe you'd let me be a fifth member of your group for a while?"

Nerf looked at Darth Susan and then back toward Milton. "I think we could use a fifth member."

I suddenly wanted to use the fake toilet nearby to do some real vomiting. I didn't know which was worse: Nerf casually letting people join their group, or Milton repeatedly saying "great dusty widgets."

"So, you'll teach me how to be a superhero?" Milton asked Nerf. "You'll show me everything you know?"

"We will," Nerf replied. "But first you . . ."

I didn't know what Nerf was going to say, and I blew my chance of finding out by deciding to change my position. As I shifted my body weight, my right hand slipped and I fell forward, causing me to whack my forehead against the edge of the bathtub. I'd like to say I was so tough that I didn't scream, but that would be the opposite of what really happened.

I saw stars and my head violently throbbed.

Darth Susan and Nerf turned and spotted me.

CHAPTER ELEVEN

Whisked Away

I wasn't sure what to do. I wasn't even sure if I was doing anything wrong. I was in a government warehouse, spying on my school secretary and her nephew. Sure, that's weird, but was it a crime? And what could an off-duty school secretary do to me? Still, my instincts told me to run. So I jumped up and dashed off in the direction I had come.

Nerf, Mud, Weasel, Millie, and Darth Susan ran after me, shouting.

I wanted to use my mediocre powers to snap off the lights, but then I wouldn't be able to see where to run. There was no way I could escape Nerf and his stooges. They were all Jocks, who prided themselves on their ability to run fast and pummel people. I was a member of the AV Club and prided myself on things like brainpower and hiding.

Hiding!

I'd been so busy running away that I had forgotten about my ability to hide. It wasn't one of my LAME gifts, but it was pretty lame, and I was gifted at it.

Twisting right, I juked and dashed behind the giant palm tree painting. Then, as quickly and clumsily as I could, I rolled under a fake log near a fake beach.

I thought of all the lights in the building going off, and instantly they did.

The sound of everyone crashing into things as the sudden darkness surprised them was more satisfying than I had anticipated. Their screaming was loud and contained a few words that the government had banned and usually sent drones out to initiate punishment.

I tried to be completely still. I only needed to stay hidden until everyone went away. Bringing my knees to my chest, I pulled myself into a tighter ball and scooted as far under the fake log as possible.

I was planning to keep still forever, but my plans were altered when someone grabbed my collar and ripped me out from under the log and up onto my feet.

"I got him," Nerf declared.

A flashlight clicked on, and its beam shone directly into my eyes.

"Mr. Dover," Darth Susan said as she held the light. I couldn't see her face or expression, but knowing her like I did, I was sure that neither one of those things was pleasant.

"What do you think you're doing?" she demanded.

"Yeah," Nerf said. "What gives?"

I held a hand up over my eyes to block out the beam of light.

"I was looking for a bathroom," I lied. "And got lost."

"Ha," Nerf said, laughing. "What a nerd. You can't even go to the bathroom right."

"Quiet," Darth Susan told him. "Why would you look for a bathroom in here, Tip?" She sounded suspicious. "And why did all the lights go out?"

I was nervous, but without missing a beat, I said, "I was

wondering the same thing about the lights. I came in here because all the government bathrooms outside have long lines. I was hoping there was a vacant one in the building. When I saw LAMER . . . I mean LAME, I couldn't help spying. They're . . ." It made me sick to say it, but I had no choice. "They're my favorite."

"Of course we are," Nerf said. "Everyone wants to look at us."

"Quiet," Darth Susan ordered her hench-boy. "You shouldn't be in here, Mr. Dover. I'm afraid it's not safe. Your bladder and curiosity are going to be the death of . . ." She paused for a moment before asking suspiciously, "Wait a second, what's that in your pocket?"

She moved the flashlight down, and I could see that some of my LAME mask was sticking out of my pocket. Instantly my pits began to sweat.

"It's my handkerchief," I lied. "I have allergies."

"Right," Darth Susan said. "And why are you dressed all in black? Let me see what that is."

I panicked. "It's my handkerchief and it's seriously gross. I've had a really snotty cold."

"I deal with you middle schoolers all day," she said. "I'm used to disgusting things."

There was no way I could show her the mask, but my options were limited. I couldn't turn off her flashlight and run, because then she would know I had powers. Plus, Nerf was holding me by the collar.

"Hand it over," she said forcefully.

I stuck my hand into my pocket while imagining what people would say at my funeral.

I was done for—the jig was up. Thanks to me, LAME was about to be exposed, and our lives would never be the same again. The government would perform tests on us and shave our heads and put us in cages until they figured out how to harness the power of our mediocre gifts.

I gulped nervously. Then there was a loud clap, and the flashlight went flying backward across the room. Nerf and I went sailing in reverse and hit the floor hard.

I couldn't see anything, and my ears were ringing. There was a brief flash of light. I felt myself being yanked by Nerf. He pulled me up and backward as Darth Susan and the others screamed things I couldn't understand.

Nerf dragged me away from the commotion and back in the direction I had come from earlier.

There were more flashes of light, and I finally realized it wasn't Nerf who was pulling me—it was Owen! I stopped struggling and began to run with him.

"What took you so long?" I yelled.

"I'm not used to this superhero stuff," he replied through his government mask.

We reached the door, and as we ran outside, I saw that Mindy and Xen had been running with us the whole time.

"Hey, you two are here!"

Brilliant deduction! Are you also aware that we're going to be dead if you don't run faster?

We sprinted at full geek-speed until we were completely out of the theater compound and safely hidden back at Owen's house. It was nice that there was no adult supervision on hand to bust us for being out. But there was a part of me that wished someone older and wiser could help us understand what the heck was going on and what we should do next.

Excuse me, you look old and wise. But mostly old.

I feel mostly annoyed. By you.

Yes, a wise voice would be helpful because our problems now seemed much larger than our current grade level.

We notified our parents that we were going to have a sleepover at Owen's, and then none of us even tried to sleep. It was more of a worry-over. We kept expecting Darth Susan and LAMER to show up and storm Owen's house. Plus, our brains were working overtime to figure out what was going on.

We knew that Darth Susan was having the Jocks dress up and pretend to be us. We knew that she had something planned for the movie's release day.

I told them about what I had overheard in the theater

warehouse and how the movie would be delivered by drone tomorrow at ten.

"So, what does it all mean?" Mindy asked.

"It makes me uneasy," Xen admitted. "I . . ." Xen burped, and the force of it knocked him across the room and onto one of the couches near the kitchen.

It's going to be okay. I mean, whatever happens, it isn't the end of the world. That's already happened.

"Right," Mindy agreed. "We have the gift of living in a time when things are so rotten that we don't have to worry about things getting worse."

Mindy had no idea how wrong she was.

CHAPTER TWELVE
Something's Missing

When morning rolled around, we debated about even going to school. But we knew that the clues and answers weren't here in Owen's house or waiting in the line for *Gritty*. They were at WADD, where Darth Susan was.

It's like when Dindo had to go into the troll trove and calm the sulking orcs just to find out who Doctavious the troll judge was trolling.

I'm still not sure I should hang out with you.

The four of us were getting a bit punchy. You never knew when you'd have to hide in uncomfortable places for long hours or fight Fanatics all night. Or if we could make it through the day without sleep.

So, we took turns cleaning up in Owen's bathroom. He let us each have fifteen seconds of sink water to clean whatever we needed. He even allowed us to use a bar of soap he had been hiding in case there was another soap shortage and he found himself in need of emergency personal hygiene.

When it was time for school, we headed out, acting as if we were prepared to take on the day. We didn't pass anyone walking to school—not a single student, Staffer, or NP. And once we reached Otto Waddle, the security hole was open and unmanned.

We crawled through the hole and discovered that the halls of our school were almost as deserted as the streets of our unfair city. I saw a couple of members of the Antisocials clique hiding behind some lockers, hoping not to stand out. I also saw a few Old-Schoolers. They were a clique that wanted nothing to do with anything that involved technology. They didn't use tablets or phones and thought electricity was a gateway luxury that led to things like indoor plumbing and ovens.

Tyler was also there sweeping the floor with a broom that was so dirty it was leaving a muddy trail as he swept.

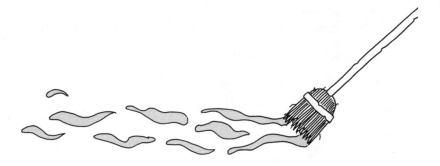

"Hey, Tyler," I said. "What gives?"

He stopped smearing mud on the floor and looked at us. "In my day, children didn't call adults by their first names," he said. "It was disrespectful to do that."

"Sorry," I apologized. "But I don't know your last name."

"And I would never tell you. You think I want you to steal my identity and all the personal trash I've amassed?"

"Okay, then," Mindy said nicely. "Do you know why the school is so empty?"

"The movie," he said. "Everyone's in line. I wanted to go, but no, the janitor doesn't get to do things that fancy middle school students do."

"We aren't in line," I pointed out.

I wouldn't expect you four to be in line, seeing how you're geeks and all.

Tyler started whistling and walked off.

At that moment, Darth Susan came driving around the

143

corner in her HTV. She pulled up in front of us and glared at me.

"You caused a mess of trouble at the theater last night, Tip," she cooed. "Such a boob."

"I—I—I—"

She interrupted my stammering. "Save the excuses, sweetie. And now look, you're here instead of waiting in line. So sad. You four don't even have the social skills to attend what is going to be the social event of the year. Coming to school while all your . . . not friends . . . not classmates . . . oh yeah, people who are about your age and live in the same area are having fun at the theater."

"We don't like those movies," Mindy said defensively.

"I don't hate them," Owen corrected her.

"How sweet. Well, now that you're here, why don't you four run off to your classes before you're marked tardy."

I looked around the empty halls in confusion.

"Why don't you just cancel school today?" I asked. "Are the Staffers even here?"

"What a bright young boy," she said sarcastically. "Like a one-watt lightbulb on its last ray. I can't just cancel school.

Education is too important. Sure, the Staffers are either waiting in line or have taken temporary jobs selling movie tickets. It turns out they can make more doing that for a few days than they can earn by working here all year."

"That doesn't seem right," Xen said.

"You're a child," Darth Susan replied. "What would you know? Now, all of you get your troublesome behinds away from me and into your classes."

"But . . ." I tried again.

I said behind, not butt! Now get! Oh, and Tip, don't think that I'm going to let last night slide. I'm working on a fitting punishment for you. Now go!

We ran down the empty halls to our classes—Mindy and Xen to theirs and Owen and me to ours.

Mr. Upwonder wasn't in class, and there was only one

145

other class member. The other student was an Old-Schooler named Hansen. He was sitting in the front row and kept scolding me and Owen every time we talked.

Be quiet! I can't hear myself worry.

I ignored Hansen and kept talking to Owen.

"The school is empty, and Darth Susan's acting like it's no big deal." I made sure I was facing him so that he could read my lips. "She's had no problem canceling school in the past. Remember when she canceled a week of school because she had spring fever?"

"Yeah," Owen said loudly.

"You have no right to be whispering," Hansen squawked. "Sit quietly."

"We have no teacher," I squawked back. "I think it's okay to talk."

I continued to whisper, knowing the world was already in pieces.

CHAPTER THIRTEEN

Figuring It Out

The rest of the day was just as odd. In my third-hour class, I was the only student.

At lunch there were only seven people in the cafeteria, and no cafeteria workers.

TODAY'S
SPECIAL

___

NONE OF YOUR
BUSINESS
WITH A SIDE
OF LEAVES

Fourth hour had four students, including me, one Old-Schooler named Byron, and two Antisocials whose names I didn't know. During class Byron began whittling something, and the Antisocials stayed at the edge of the room trying to blend in with the wall.

Ten minutes into class the door opened.

Darth Susan came in, followed by the Pep Liaison and a tall gentleman wearing a dark blue uniform and holding a clipboard. All three stared at us.

I raised my hand, but nobody acknowledged me.

The fact that the Pep Liaison was here made me uneasy. After all, he had been part of the problem a couple of months back when we saved the school. Even though he always smiled, he was never to be trusted.

"And you say these numbers are normal for your school?" the dark-suited man asked.

"Perfectly normal," Darth Susan said as she glared at me and my raised hand. "Plus, the few students who do come are unimpressive and nothing to celebrate."

"Celebrations are a shameful waste of time," Byron the Old-Schooler said as he whittled.

The dark-suited man looked at Byron and coughed uncomfortably.

I've seen enough. Show me some other rooms.

"Of course," Darth Susan said.

She then ushered the blue-suited man out of our class-room while scowling at me. When the door was closed, I hopped up and pushed my face against the small window and looked out into the hall.

I saw Darth Susan and her pathetic posse disappear down the hall in the HTV.

"What is going on?" I said aloud.

"It's not any of our business," Byron said. "And I'm glad of it. Minding my own business is one of the few pleasures I'm allowed to enjoy."

The two Antisocials in the room just stood there blushing.

I know that my friends and I are socially awkward. Sure, we don't often fit in or stand out, and people overlook us and make fun of us. We have bad style, out-of-date hair, and only one another as followers on all social media. Still, I have to say that compared to the Old-Schoolers and the Antisocials, we are downright *with it* and *outgoing*.

"I'm leaving," I told them.

"In my day, we never left class early," Byron said.

"This *is* your day," I reminded him. "We're the same age."

I left the room and walked down Q Hall, keeping my eyes peeled for any sign of the HTV. I knew Mindy was in Senseless Economics, so I headed there and peered through the window on the classroom door.

She was sitting alone and staring at the chalkboard. I entered her one-person class and took a seat beside her.

"That's where Scott McLaughlin sits," she said.

"Well, it looks like he's not here today," I replied. "Did Darth Susan come by?"

"Yes, with Peppy and some tall blue guy." Mindy sounded both bored and fed up at the same time. "They took a class count and then started talking about how nobody values education anymore. The blue guy also said something about acting fair, or a fairness act."

A bell went off in my head!

Some of my favorite informational things to read are books and articles about how the government works. Last week I finished a two-hundred-page article about the legal system in Piggsburg and how the town spends the money the government gives it. For the record—not wisely. The week before that I read a paper on NinCon Troopers and the different ranks they can have. And the week before that I read a paper on census taking and how the government keeps track of people in various areas and regions by conducting censuses.

The most riveting part of the census paper was about education and how the government keeps track of the students in school. They use census information to further control everyone.

"The Fairness Act!" I shouted.

"What?" Mindy asked.

"I can't believe I was so blind."

"Blind?" Mindy said. "Like after the time you ate that glowing pudding?"

"Yes, but the blindness I'm talking about now might not be temporary. The Fairness Act is what they call the education census rule. The government does surprise inspections to get a count of how many students are attending a school. But since it's unfair to judge a school's attendance by just one day, the Fairness Act requires the government to get a second day's sampling and average the two numbers."

You're putting me to sleep.

But don't you see?

Yes, you're the blind one, remember?

"No," I shouted. "They're counting our school numbers, and because everyone's waiting in line for the movie, we have next to none. If our second-day numbers are anything like today's, we are doomed. According to the Fairness Act, if a school has two days of less than twenty-five percent attendance, it's in danger of being shut down. If it has two days of less than ten percent, it is to be shut down immediately and all students and staff shipped off to other schools or outposts."

"Or in Darth Susan's case," Mindy said, finally catching on, "she will be offered an early retirement and be free of her job forever while we suffer at outpost #72."

"Exactly! She'll win and finally get what she wanted before we stopped her two months ago."

Owen and Xen burst through the door and into the classroom.

"I heard everything," Owen informed us.

"I didn't," Xen said.

"I also just heard Peppy tell Darth Susan in secret that the second count is scheduled for tomorrow."

It looked like the fight to avoid outpost #72 and ruin Darth Susan's day was heating up once again. As we brainstormed about what to do, it was Xen who struck upon the one idea that just might work. It was a wild idea, and the odds of success were a billion to one.

I stared at Owen. "What did you say?"

"Great fussy widgets," he answered. "Milton MacDuffin says it all the time."

"You know Milton?" I asked.

"Everyone knows Milton." Owen looked at me like I was an idiot. "He only starred in the third movie."

"Wait!" I said with fervor. "Darth Susan's nephew, the one she was talking to in the theater prop house, was named Milton. He was the one who kept using that dumb saying."

"Milton MacDuffin is related to Darth Susan?" Owen was beside himself.

That's how she knew when the movie was going to come out.

"She used the fake LAME to trick Milton into giving her the information," Xen said.

"And she bribed Peppy so that he would schedule the surprise counts on the two days that she knew nobody would be here," Owen added.

"She's the worst!" I said needlessly.

None of us could argue with that.

"Well," I said loudly, "it looks like it's up to us to ruin things for her. Which means we've got a job to do."

Ready, set, LAME!

Sadly, there wasn't time to stop and point out how bad Xen's tagline was.

LAME was on the move.

CHAPTER FOURTEEN
Paper Jam

The first step in our somewhat-genius plan required paper. Not a couple of pieces of paper but hundreds and hundreds of pieces. Procuring the goods wasn't going to be easy. These days paper was a hot commodity. When teachers get their hands on any, they protect it with their lives.

At WADD, teachers fight for paper. Darth Susan and the Jocks won most of it during the Supply War. But when the teachers got it, they would hoard and hide it. We had heard rumors about them hiding a magical mountain of paper under an Arm-ageddon chair in the Staffers' asylum. Armageddon chairs were blocky and typically made of concrete or something strong to help the chair keep its shape in the event of Armageddon. The chairs were usually covered with some fabric or blankets to make them a little more comfortable to sit on.

The Staffers' asylum was sort of like a teachers' lounge but with less hope. It was a room where teachers went to recover from headaches or eat one of the lousy selections from the vending machine.

The Staffers' asylum was four doors down from the office. We were able to break into it without much trouble.

Mindy only needed to click her fingers to send a small shock wave that shattered the doorknob.

"Your clicks are as strong as your claps," Xen said in awe.

"Thanks. I've been practicing."

Inside were a table with wood chairs that didn't match, a TV that didn't work, a microwave, a vending machine, two couches, and one Arm-ageddon chair. Owen took a seat.

For a while now we had heard that the teachers hid all their paper under the Arm-ageddon chair. Darth Susan never came into the Staffers' asylum, so they felt it was a safe place.

Owen got up, and Mindy grabbed the edge of the blanket and pulled it off the top of the chair. Instantly we could see that the stories were beyond true. The paper wasn't under the chair. It *was* the chair.

Great fussy widgets!

My friends looked at me like I had lost my mind.

"What? I don't want to say it," I argued. "It's stuck in my head like a bad song."

"Well, sing it to yourself," Mindy said.

I grabbed two reams of paper that were currently helping to form the Arm-ageddon chair's right arm. Mindy then threw the blanket back over it.

It was now up to Xen to work his magic. Designing things wasn't one of Xen's LAME gifts. He was good at it long before we were bitten by spiders. Xen had designed our LAME logo and most of the creative things the AV Club had used in the past. Now he needed to design a flyer that would potentially ruin Darth Susan's plans and prevent us from having to attend outpost number #72.

A well-designed flyer can change the world.

Xen sat down at the table and went to work. As soon as he was done, we took the flyer and the paper and prepared ourselves for what would probably be the hardest part of our plan. There was no way around it—we were going to the library.

We left the teachers' asylum and walked down the hall in a group as Owen listened for lizards and secretaries.

"You know no one is ever going to realize what we've done to save this place," Mindy said forlornly.

"Bums me out too." Owen sighed. "I would love people to stop thinking we're only good at things like sudoku and computers."

"Yeah," Xen said. "I'd like someone to invite me to play beat ball without me having to be the beat."

"It's not going to happen," I informed them. "But luckily, middle school isn't forever. In a couple of years we'll be in high school and we'll be getting ignored there instead."

We walked down the hall and made it past the office, and then we headed toward the kingdom of Mrs. Shh. She possessed the one thing we needed most. Our plan couldn't go forward until we'd tricked her into letting us use it. We were hoping she would be gone today, but Owen could hear her inside the library, taping books closed.

"If this goes wrong, Mrs. Shh will kill us," Mindy whispered. "Last time I saw her, she swatted me with a book about manners because she thought it would make me less sarcastic. Then she yelled at me for having dark hair. I guess one of her cats has dark hair, and the cat has been giving her attitude lately."

We reached the library doors and stood there for a moment. Tyler had fixed them, and they were now back in place and locked.

There was a lot on the line. And I just wasn't sure that the League of Average and Mediocre Entities could pull this off.

Despite my lack of confidence, it was time to disturb the queen.

CHAPTER FIFTEEN

Snappy Solutions

Darth Susan is the most feared person at WADD. For a school secretary, she's done a good job of rising to the top. The second-most feared person isn't Principal Woth. In fact, he doesn't even register on the scare scale.

No, the second-most feared is Mrs. Shh. Not because she's the librarian and refuses to share her books without a battle—a fact that makes her a first-round ballot for the Horrible Human Hall of Fame. Or because she is the inventor of the Very Dismal System. What gives Mrs. Shh the most power is that she controls the copy machine. Nobody can touch it without her blessing.

The reason the copy machine is in the library is because a while back Mrs. Shh had gone head-to-head with Darth Susan over who got the best parking space. Darth Susan won by accidentally having Mrs. Shh's car smashed by a wrecking-havoc ball.

Mrs. Shh wasn't too happy about that. So at the beginning of last year, she broke into the office and stole the old beat-up-and-tied-together copy machine.

Then she made a dam of books in front of the doorway to prevent anyone from being able to get to it.

Eventually the dam burst when a couple of Sox slid into it, but nobody tried to take the machine back. Even Darth Susan knew that it was a battle she couldn't win. So the copy machine stayed in the library. Now anyone who needs to make a copy must beg and plead.

And getting permission to make copies was almost impossible. First of all, you have to BYOP (bring your own paper) and offer Mrs. Shh gifts—things like cat treats for her cats, or interesting buttons.

Yeah, that's right: Mrs. Shh loves buttons. I can't explain it, and please don't make me. She's just one of those grown-ups who does things that don't make any sense.

Our plan to use the copier required a sacrificial pawn, and Xen had reluctantly agreed to be it. He was the only one of us who hadn't had a run-in with Mrs. Shh. Plus, he wanted to see if he was a good enough actor to pull off the lie he was going to have to tell.

So Xen stood in front of the library door while me, Mindy, and Owen hid inside empty lockers nearby and looked out the slots. Once we were set, Xen knocked. A few seconds later I could see Mrs. Shh's eye staring out at him through the peephole.

After what felt like my entire lifetime, she threw open the door.

The library is closed. You need to leave immediately, before I am forced to fine you for breathing on my books without my permission.

"I have asthma," Xen told her. "I only breathe through my nose."

"Well then, I'll fine you for sniffing in the books," she said.

"Okay, I just thought you might be able to tell me what a six-holed pearl-plated flat button is. I'll get someone else to look."

"What did you say?" she demanded while grabbing Xen by the shoulders and looking him in the eyes.

"Nothing," Xen said, acting (or maybe *not* acting) nervous. "Someone found a six-holed pearl-plated flat button outside."

"Impossible," Mrs. Shh told him. "Impossible."

"Right. Sorry to bother you."

"Wait!"

Mrs. Shh stepped all the way out of the library and glared down at Xen. I could see that his knees were knocking and he was trying hard not to burp.

"Do you think I'm dumb?" she asked.

I made a silent wish that Xen wouldn't be as honest as he usually was.

Xen shook his head.

"I see what you're doing. You want to keep the button to yourself, don't you?"

"Actually . . ."

"Nice try. Do you think I was born yesterday?"

Xen shook his head again. It was easy for him to be honest about that question. Nobody thought Mrs. Shh was born yesterday. She looked older than at least a couple of thousand yesterdays.

"Well, it's not going to work." Mrs. Shh pulled the library door closed and locked it. "Now show me that button."

Xen turned on his feet and marched back down the hall with Mrs. Shh following him.

Once they were out of sight, we slipped from the lockers and up to the library door.

Xen pulled it off.

So far, so terrifying.

Mindy clapped her hands, and the entire doorframe and door broke from the wall and came falling down. We threw our arms up to stop the door from crushing us.

The door almost smashed us, but we were able to shift our hold and set it down softly on the floor. We ran into the library and headed for the copy machine. Owen pulled open the large tray and put both reams of paper in. Mindy slapped the flyer Xen had made down onto the copier, and I used my gift to bypass the starting code and get the machine powered up. Instantly the copier began spitting out copies of Xen's flyer.

"How much time do you think we have?" Mindy asked.

"Xen's going to lead her to the football field while pretending to look for the button," I answered. "When Mrs. Shh discovers there's no button, she'll probably come right back."

"I can hear them exiting the school," Owen said. "They're near the burned-out shed, and Mrs. Shh is telling Xen that toggles are just wannabe buttons."

"Poor Xen," Mindy said. "I would—"

All three of us jumped. Owen had been so busy listening to Xen that he had failed to hear Tyler coming in through the broken door and walking right up to us.

I glanced at Mindy and she glanced at me as the copier continued to print out our flyers.

Owen was the only one of us with enough composure to answer.

"We were looking for Mrs. Shh. The door was knocked down, and we came in here to see where she was."

"That makes no sense," Tyler said suspiciously. "Why would any student be looking for the librarian?"

Tyler was right. Here at WADD, the librarian wasn't someone most kids wanted to find on purpose.

Now I know you're lying. You'd better come with me.

"That's okay," I said nicely. "How about we just go back to our class?"

"That would be easier for me," Tyler agreed. "But I have my orders to report anything suspicious, and you three standing in a place like the library seems suspicious. Follow me."

The three of us followed Tyler out of the library as the copier continued to print our flyers. We stepped over the broken door, and Tyler grumbled.

"Did you kids have something to do with this?"

"No," Mindy said.

"This whole school is a piece of junk," he complained. "Someone should be embarrassed."

It seemed weird that Tyler was complaining, seeing how he was the one in charge of school maintenance.

"You four sure have been a lot of trouble lately."

Tyler looked us over as we walked, and he realized there were only three of us.

"Where's that other one? The short one who wears books on his feet? Did he wise up and join a better group? Maybe the Scrums or the Blotches?"

"You think we're worse than the Scrums and the Blotches?" Mindy asked angrily.

"Susan is going to have a field day with you," Tyler said. "She might have to enforce her right as a general-secretary and lock you three in detention for a week."

"She can't do that," Mindy argued.

"You might be surprised."

We couldn't afford to be locked up. Our plan to save the very school that might soon lock us up would be ruined if we were detained in any way. I looked around for something to turn on or off. It was up to me to fix this mess. I was the one who—

Mindy snapped her fingers while flinging them up toward Tyler's head. The force of her snap sent his trash can helmet spinning wildly. Tyler started to scream as the movement of the twisting can sent him bouncing into the walls like an out-of-control top. Mindy started using both hands to fling clicks directly toward Tyler and keep him moving farther down the hall. He was screaming and trying to stop himself, but the movement of his head kept him off-balance and unable to regain his footing.

"What are you doing?" I yelled at Mindy.

I wasn't too worried about Tyler hearing me, since he was busy spinning and screaming.

"We had to do something," Mindy said. "We can't get caught now."

"Where's Xen?" I asked Owen.

He listened for a single second. "He's in back of the school telling Mrs. Shh that it must not have been a button he saw. She's not happy about it."

"Okay," I said. "We don't have much time. Run to the library, get the flyers, and then get out. Mindy will keep Tyler spinning, and I'll find Xen. Let's all meet at Owen's house as soon as we can."

"This is crazy," Mindy said as she clicked.

Owen took off.

Tyler kept spinning.

I went to save Xen. Well, I went to save Xen right after making a quick stop at the office. There was something I needed to get.

CHAPTER SIXTEEN
High Flyers

It turns out that Xen didn't need saving. By the time I reached him, Mrs. Shh had already reprimanded him for the fake button news and returned to the library. Xen and I left the mostly abandoned school and ran to Owen's house.

We worried about Mindy and Owen for a few minutes before they both showed up. Owen had all the flyers in his arms.

"We did it," he said in amazement.

"We did part of it," I reminded him. "So far we've just made some flyers. I miss the good old days when things like making copies wasn't a survival-type activity. How do they look?"

Owen handed me one.

THE SAND THROWER SERIES

GRiTTY
THE MOVIE

Showing today @ 11 a.m. at
OTTO WADDLE JR. HIGH
GOVERNMENT OUTPOST

Piggsburg's
only showing

ADMISSION IS FREE

#PEACETHROUGHMOVIES #NOSPOILERS
#BOOKSAREBETTER #MOVIESAREBETTER

"It's not my fanciest design," Xen said. "But I calculate our plan as having a thirty-two percent chance of working."

"I one hundred percent knew you would say that."

We went over the plan a dozen more times and then returned to our own homes for the night. We needed to sleep and be ready for what could be the biggest day of our lives.

At dinner my parents couldn't stop talking about tomorrow's movie opening.

They wanted me to skip school and go wait in line with them. When I told them that I needed to go to school, they seemed disappointed.

Falling asleep was surprisingly easy, and before I knew it, morning had arrived. I got up and got ready as quickly as I could. I put on my LAME suit and wore a large jacket over it.

My parents had already left to go wait in line at the theater compound, so the house was empty. I went into our emergency-preparedness room and grabbed the inflatable life raft. My dad had bought it a while back, when the government had been talking about flooding Piggsburg in hopes of washing away some of the many smells.

After getting the raft, I went to the kitchen and grabbed some stale crackers for breakfast. I choked them down, gathered my things, and left for Xen's.

When I arrived, my friends were already there. They all had their costumes on, hidden under their coats.

We put on our pollution masks and then began the hike across town to the government drone ease-way on the other side of the dry lake. On the way there, we passed WADD and saw that it looked completely vacant.

"I hope this works," Mindy said.

Xen groaned. "I hope we don't get arrested and have to work the government waste-mines for the rest of our lives."

"Yeah, that too," Xen agreed.

The ease-way we were walking to was on the far end of the dry lake. It was created as a place where drones could fly without interference. Ease-ways were like freeways for flying things, long strips of barren land with nothing on them so that drones could zip over the earth without too many people throwing sticks or spears at them. People still did, but since the ease-ways were outside the neighborhoods and main parts of the city, the drones were a little less likely to get messed with.

Well, we were going to mess with one today.

We circled around the edge of the dry lake and tromped through some tall, ragged pine trees. We stepped over a broken fence and arrived at a section of ease-way seventeen that was hidden by trees. Mindy knew about the spot because her older brother came here occasionally to set off fireworks.

I tried to sound confident as I said, "According to what Milton told Darth Susan, the drone's going to pass overhead shortly."

"You're putting a lot of trust in this Milton kid." Mindy shook her head as she talked. "What if he's wrong?"

"Well, then we can prepare to live a pummel-rich life at outpost #72."

I pulled out the inflatable raft and yanked the cord on the side of it. In seconds it was completely inflated. We positioned the puffy yellow boat in the middle of the ease-way and threw our jackets into it for extra padding.

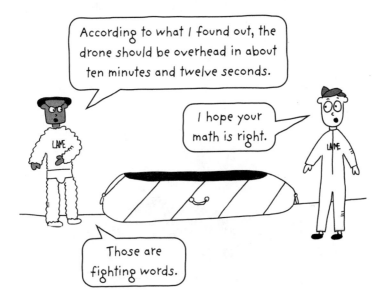

Nine minutes later we saw a government drone coming over the horizon. Mindy and Xen pushed the raft into the perfect position to be directly in line with the oncoming drone. They fluffed up our coats, and Owen did some math in his head to calculate the exact moment I would need to shut things off.

"Five, four, three, two, now!" he said.

I thought about the drone shutting down, and it dropped from the sky, still falling forward as it did. Owen's calculations were right on, and the drone landed in the jacket-filled raft.

There wasn't a second to waste.

Mindy snapped open the metal lock on the top of the drone and pulled out a black flash drive. I took the one I had

188

borrowed from Darth Susan's office and popped it into the
drone. Mindy closed the compartment, and we all stood up
and backed away from the raft.

The drone rose and continued forward on its pro-
grammed flight as if four geeks hadn't just messed with it.

"Amazing," Xen whispered. "I can't believe that worked."

"Me neither," I said.

We all wanted to stand around and be impressed with
ourselves, but the clock was ticking. We put our coats back
on and took off, leaving the raft behind. There was no time
to deflate it or drag it behind us. We were already late for
school.

When we got to WADD, Owen listened in.

"I can't hear anyone in there besides Darth Susan and Tyler," Owen reported. "Darth Susan is driving the HTV down the far hall and laughing. Tyler is in the cafeteria eating something and mumbling about how disgusting it is."

We slipped through the vacant security hole and made our way to the audiovisual room behind the stage in the auditorium.

"Time?" I asked Mindy.

"You have a watch," she said.

"I know, it just sounds cooler if you tell me. Time?"

"Ten thirty-four," she said, being a good sport.

We quickly hooked up the flash drive and all the equipment and monitors we needed. We wanted to make sure that everything was in place to broadcast the movie to all the classrooms that had connections. Using the technology at our school was always a risk. Sometimes it didn't work, and if it did work, there was always the possibility that it would break down. We were hoping that today we would have no problems. We only needed it to work for a short while.

With everything hooked up, we climbed the ladder near

the postapocalyptic art room and stepped out onto the roof of the school.

Finn was away, leaving his tower empty.

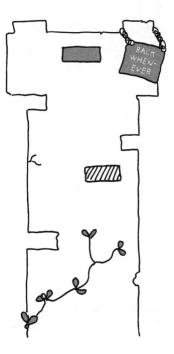

Owen and I unfolded the emergency weather balloon he had taken from his dad. Owen's father collected them so that he could someday build a bathtub balloon ship to transport his family to someplace less nuts.

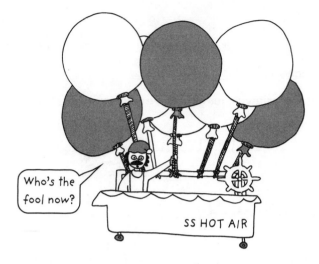

Xen pulled out a huge bottle of fizzy seltzer water that he had added baking soda to. He took off the cap and drank like there was no tomorrow, which was appropriate seeing how there would be no tomorrow if we failed.

"Sorry," I said. "But we need your belches to be extraordinary."

Mindy and Owen unfolded the giant balloon and began shoving the flyers we had made into the open end. I took a marker and quickly wrote something on the side of it.

Xen finished his drink and started jumping up and down to get his gut working. In no time at all he began to burp. We held the balloon's opening toward him and he aimed his belches directly into it. It only took one and a half super-burps to fill the massive balloon and almost knock us all off the roof.

It wasn't easy, but Mindy and I quickly tied it closed with some rope.

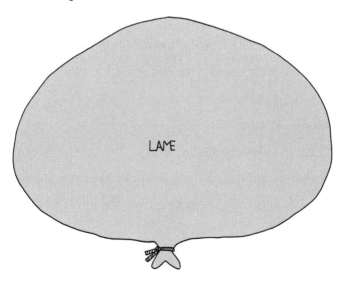

Owen and I struggled to lift and push the balloon up on Finn's tower.

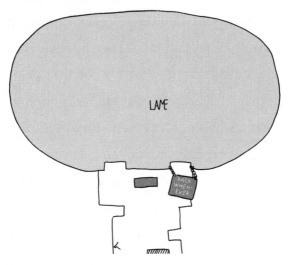

Xen directed his mouth up toward the fully inflated balloon and got to burping.

Xen kept at it and the balloon shot up off the tower and into the sky at an impressive rate.

"Time!" I shouted.

"Ten forty-two."

"Listen!" Owen yelled.

None of us needed Owen's super hearing to hear the angry roars and screams coming from the south. Their voices rose up in the sky just like the balloon we had launched. The movie was supposed to have started a few minutes ago, but everyone at the theaters had just discovered that the flash drive the theaters were using didn't have *Gritty* on it. It had something much more terrible.

"What was on that flash drive?" Mindy asked.

"Home movies of Darth Susan and her lizard on their trip to the Minnesota trash pyramids."

"Ewwww!" the distant crowd screamed.

"They probably just saw the part where she was giving her lizard, Becky, a good-night kiss," I said with concern.

"What have we done?" Owen whispered somberly.

The noise of a disappointed and disgusted crowd grew louder and louder.

I glanced up and saw the weather balloon. It looked miles away now, and it was drifting to the south and toward the theater compound.

"Too late to turn back now," I said loudly. "Do it, Mindy!"

Mindy looked up at the sky and aimed her hands toward the distant balloon. She braced her legs and pulled back her arms.

"Ready?" she said with a nervous smile.

Owen, Xen, and I all nodded.

Mindy thrust her arms forward and brought her hands together with a tremendous *crack!* Owen and I were blown off our feet and onto our backs next to Xen. The sound of the clap shot through the sky with unbelievable force. Up in the

air the weather balloon exploded just as Mindy had wanted
it to. There was an eruption of paper in the sky above us.

"It worked," Owen said in disbelief.

We stood there and watched the flyers rain down over
the polluted skyline of Piggsburg. The wind was moving
them like a blanket of rectangular snow all over the city.

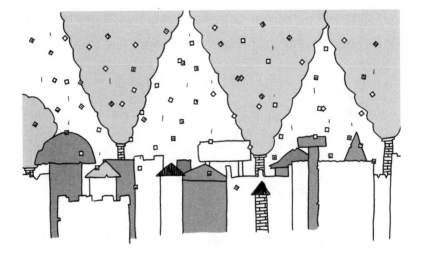

"Places!" I yelled.

We scrambled off the roof and back down to the AV room so that we could do some intense waiting.

The plan was well in motion.

Now there was nothing to do but wait (and think of all the things that could still go wrong).

CHAPTER SEVENTEEN

Confrontation

The Pep Liaison and the district census counter were scheduled to be at WADD at eleven. We calculated that based on wind speed and the distance, it would take 1.3 minutes for the first of the flyers to drift down to earth. But we were wrong. Once the balloon had burst, the flyers flew quickly in all directions. Owen could hear people all over the city reading them aloud. Anyone coming from the theater compound would be here in approximately fifteen minutes. The flyers were landing everywhere, which meant that some people would be here much sooner.

Owen kept a constant ear to the wind. There was so much excitement and chaos that his head rocked back and forth as he listened.

They're coming! I can hear people only a few blocks away.

"Great!" I said happily.

"Not really," Owen shouted. "There's a problem. Darth Susan is onto us."

"What?" I asked.

"Someone caught one of the flyers and phoned her. They read her what it says. Also LAMER is here. Darth Susan is screaming at them about how someone's trying to ruin her no-count."

"Cratch!" I swore passionately. "I hope LAMER's not able to thwart our plan."

Mindy stared at me. I couldn't tell for sure, but she looked super impressed with my passionate state of mind and my cool choice of words.

"Thwart?" she asked sarcastically.

"What?" I said defensively. "It's a good word, and I've always wanted to use it."

"Well," Owen piped up. "They are going to thwart our plans because Darth Susan and LAMER just reached the front of the school. They are currently outside the security hole stopping people from coming in."

Xen moaned. "I didn't calculate this happening."

"Okay, okay," I said, trying to think. "We can do this. In fact, this might help."

"Help?" Mindy asked. "How?"

"By help, I mean help our street cred." I tried to look as serious as I could. "You guys know what we've got to do, right?"

We all looked at each other.

"Let's take on LAMER," Xen said.

Mindy smiled. "I was hoping it would come to this."

"Well . . ." Owen gulped. "I was worried it would."

"This is our moment!" I cheered. "We get to show LAMER what it means to be LAME!"

The four of us ran out of the AV room and climbed back up onto the roof. We thought it would look cool, and blow everyone's minds, to descend from the front of the school and land right on top of LAMER. But when we got to the edge of the roof and looked down at the drop, we suddenly got cold feet.

Not only was the drop a bit higher than we remembered, but down below us, all four members of LAMER were blocking the security hole.

Darth Susan pulled the HTV up behind them and in front of the hole, creating an even bigger obstacle for anyone who might try to get in.

There was a rapidly growing crowd of normal citizens who had seen Xen's flyer and came over. They were itching to get inside and see the movie. It was now playing all over the world but Piggsburg was missing out.

The Fanatics and Normals were jittery and anxious to get in.

Darth Susan scowled as she sat on the HTV and looked out at the growing crowd. It would take a miracle to stop people from entering, and all she had was LAMER.

She leaned over from her seat and whispered something to Nerf. He listened for a moment while shaking. This wasn't a football game or a Supply War. This was something much bigger than anything he had ever punched or bullied his way out of.

Darth Susan finished whispering and Nerf stepped closer to the crowd. He held up his hands and shouted at the huge group of movie-hungry people.

Stay back! For the safety of all man-, woman-, and person-kind. You must not enter the school. It is cursed. All who enter will lose likes and lives.

It seemed impossible to believe, but the amped-up mob was obeying him. Nerf was holding back a large wave of desperate moviegoers by pretending to be us and lying about a curse. Although I guess in some way our entire world was cursed.

Darth Susan sat on her HTV looking like an evil puppet master who was smugly enjoying what her fake-puppet super-group was doing.

"What now?" Owen asked. "Nobody's going in. Will they still be counted as members of our school if they're outside?"

"No." I took a moment to properly moan. "According to the bylaws of the census, the humans have to be inside the actual building for them to be counted."

Darth Susan motioned Nerf over and whispered something else to him. Nerf then turned and relayed the message to the crowd.

"She . . . I mean we suggest you all go home to avoid any further cursing."

Remarkably, it looked like the crowd was thinking about obeying him!

They were still jittery and anxious, but because he was wearing a superhero costume and talking about a curse, some of them were beginning to turn away.

Wait! I don't want you to go. You should stay around. Sit out here and stare at us.

Nerf started to flex his muscles and show off.

Our plan was falling apart right before our eyes. Everything came down to this moment, and this moment was crumbling. We were just four Geeks up on a roof and out of answers.

"I guess I'll need to start bulking up," Xen whispered.

"What?" Mindy asked.

"I know I can belch for protection, but it's probably a good idea to work out a little before we're shipped off to outpost #72."

Owen shivered. "I heard the principal is an ex-con, ex-cop, and current carney."

"No one's going to 72," Mindy promised. "The district census counter will be here in ten minutes. So, we just need to remove some ugly blockage from the front of the security hole."

"Um," Xen said. "I've calculated our odds of defeating LAMER, and it's ninety eight point four percent. But if the crowd jumps in and helps them, our odds decrease dramatically."

"We have no choice," I whispered. "If we don't try, we only have ourselves to LAME."

Everyone groaned.

Mindy stood up straight and glanced around. We could all hear and see the crowd growing below. The moment seemed monumental.

"This isn't a time for bad puns," Mindy said. "This is a time for action."

Looking down over the edge, Mindy threw her hands together and clapped. The flagpole in front of the school cracked at the base and fell swiftly toward the school. It hit the edge of the roof with a *thwack* and created the perfect sliding pole.

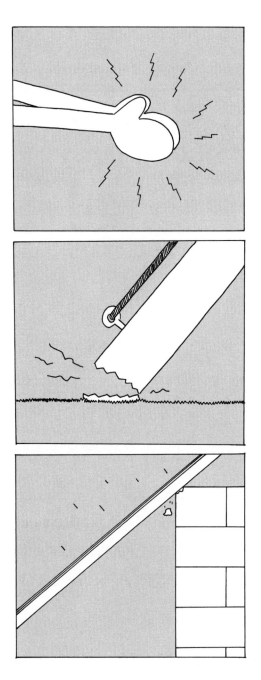

CRACK!

CREEECH!

CRUNCH!

Without saying a word, all four of us straddled the pole and slid down to where the action was.

It happened so fast that the crowd didn't know what was going on or how to react. But suddenly, in a flash, we were standing on the ground in front of LAMER and Darth Susan. The mob of people looked . . . confused.

"What the hero?" someone in the crowd yelled.

Darth Susan didn't miss a beat. She pointed at us and screamed . . .

Get those impostors!

The growing crowd seemed more than willing to do her bidding. They started to yell the sort of things that courteous crowds never would. It was a terrifying sight—Fanatics and Normals all hopped up on mob mentality and stomping toward us.

I quickly thought of everyone's phone ringing, and all phones in the area went off. The noise created a circus of sound and confusion. Some of the Fanatics were mad.

"They did it!" Nerf yelled while pointing at us.

The crowd raged with anger and closed in around us.

"This is the end," Owen said.

"No, it's not," Mindy shouted. "Quick, Xen, what is the gash of X times the square root of five divided by the number of errors in the Very Dismal System?"

Xen looked stunned. "That's impossible . . . there's too many . . ."

Xen rocked back and forth. He couldn't calculate the incalculable equation. His head shook, and with one giant nuclear burp, he belched.

BWUFFT!

Everyone went down!

Well, not everyone at once. Nerf flew straight up about five feet before coming down. It was too bad that there weren't any Fanatics still standing to take a picture of him flying.

Everyone moaned and muttered as they struggled to get back onto their feet. I stood and pulled Owen up next to me as the massive gathering of people worked their way back on their feet.

Our evil school secretary had been blown off the HTV. She got up fuming. Nerf and his poser friends stood up next to her looking baffled and wobbly. Darth Susan pinched Nerf on the arm and screamed, "Get them!"

Nerf looked scared.

"You heard her," he said to Mud, Weasel, and Millie. "Get them."

Nerf stepped back while his three friends came at us. Mindy took Millie down with a single sonic snap. Owen and I charged Mud and Weasel. We didn't have super-strength, but we had moves. Seconds before we barreled into them, Xen burped and they flew backward as if we had just blown them over. It was a bit of trickery, but it made us look more powerful than we were.

"Hey!" a Fanatic in the crowd yelled, and pointed. "They're not the impostors. They are!"

"No," Nerf said. "We're the real heroes. We—"

Before he could finish his lie, Owen lunged forward and flashed him with his eyes.

Nerf was temporarily blinded, so I took the moment to jump up and ram his legs.

"The HTV!" Mindy yelled while pointing to where it was parked in front of the security hole. "Get that rope from the flagpole!"

Owen pulled the rope off the broken flagpole and tossed one end of it to Mindy. She ran around LAMER and Darth Susan as Owen flashed his eyes at them and Xen burped just enough to keep them off balance. The crowd was clapping and cheering as if the movie had already begun.

Mindy cinched the rope around them, and we all quickly tied them to the HTV.

Instead of releasing them, we decided to pull the masks off LAMER.

Nerf and his friends were finally exposed.

The crowd cheered and booed.

It was a nice moment for geeks everywhere. The forces who had messed with us for so long were getting their come-uppance.

We weren't going to let them go, but we *were* going to let

them go away. Normally the HTV required the key that Darth Susan wore around her neck, but starting engines was what I was best at.

I imagined the cart engine turned on. I pushed the stick into drive, and the HTV started to move away from the school and toward Elm Street. The crowd parted, and all five bullies slowly rolled away, yelling and screaming.

The ever-growing crowd of Fanatics and Normals looked at us. There were so many of them now that I couldn't take them all in with one glance.

"Sorry about those impostors," I shouted. "They wanted you to miss the movie. We want you to see it. Show starts in four minutes."

The cheering was so loud I thought my eardrums would burst.

We motioned everyone toward the security hole, and they began to file in, pushing each other through the hole as fast as they could. A bunch of Fanatics broke the locked doors nearby, allowing even more people to stream into the building. The four of us stood back and watched the river of humanity flow into our once-vacant school.

Do you think LAMER and Darth will be okay? I mean, they're tied to the HTV going almost two miles an hour.

"I can hear them screaming," Owen reported. "They're slowly rolling down Elm Street. They're angry but fine."

"And I'll turn off the HTV as soon as they're far enough away."

I heard someone clearing his throat and turned to find the Pep Liaison and a woman with thick glasses and a blue sweater. She said her name was Elaine Simplot.

Excuse me, this is Elaine Simplot from the district.

What is happening here? I demand to see your principal.

"He's teaching some new students how to survive by hiding," I lied. "But he asked us to show you in."

"Who are you?" Elaine said with a sniff.

"This is LAME," Peppy answered for us. "They saved me from ruin a couple of months back. You can trust them."

I don't trust children. I'm here to take a count of those inside and nothing else.

Elaine followed us into the school, and we let her do her job. It wasn't easy—she could barely move through the hall due to all the people. She tried to go into a couple of class-rooms, but there wasn't an inch of extra space.

"Time?" I whispered to Mindy.

"We have two minutes," she whispered back.

There was way more of the school for Elaine to view, but she was bothered by the crowd and could clearly see that our student population was off the charts.

This school's attendance is above bursting. Get me out of here. I'm done!

We gladly escorted Ms. Simplot and Peppy out the front and off the campus. As they walked away, we could see hundreds of people still streaming into the school.

"Did we do it?" Xen asked excitedly.

"I think we—"

"Look out!" Mindy yelled.

Running toward us at a breakneck speed was a disheveled-looking Darth Susan. She was coming up the street and holding what looked like a piece of the HTV. She swung it wildly above her head while screaming.

Feel the wrath of an angry secretary!

Darth Susan swung the piece of HTV directly down toward my head. It had all happened so fast that I couldn't move. Luckily, my friends could. Mindy clapped and Xen burped simultaneously in Darth Susan's direction, creating a burp-clap cloud.

Darth Susan flew back and into a bush across the street. She was defeated. She looked as if she had been put through the ringer and chewed up by life. I almost felt sorry for her. She struggled in the bush and then cried out.

Xen was very happy to answer her.

"Not bad," I told Xen.

Darth Susan fell to her knees and beat the ground with her fists.

The four of us turned away from her. We joined the stream of people moving into the school and miraculously got the movie started on time.

CHAPTER EIGHTEEN

Down and Nerdy

The movie was fine. It didn't seem like anyone really hated it, and nobody really loved it. Worldwide everyone thought it was just okay.

GRITTY: THE MOVIE

REVIEWED BY ED BLANCH OF SUSDSA TODAY

I think it was good. This movie didn't make me mad or make me happy.

It was okay, all right, fine, acceptable, and whatever.

If you're looking for a movie that exists, this movie is for you.

** 1/2

TWO AND A HALF STARS

Fanatics didn't hate it enough to throw a fit. A weird kind of peace settled over Piggsburg and the world.

How long it would last nobody could tell.

For the record, most of the AV Club thought the movie was awful. Owen did like how it wrapped up Ky-Ryder's story.

Nerf, Mud, Weasel, and Millie eventually made it back to school—the HTV did not. It had run into a tree near the dry lake and broke apart.

Right after the movie was shown at our school, we took the flash drive to the theater compound and secretly dropped it off. Because of demand, the government ran the movie nonstop in every theater for the past two weeks straight. Because of no-demand, they never ran a second screening of Darth Susan and Becky's vacation to the trash pyramids in the State Formerly Known as Minnesota.

According to the census count Ms. Simplot took, our school was two hundred and thirty-seven percent filled to capacity. Because of that the district not only planned to keep it open, but they planned to hire an assistant principal to work under Principal Woth.

Darth Susan was devastated. After all, there was a good chance that the assistant principal might take away some of her control. Plus, her plan to shut down our school had miserably failed. Once again LAME had messed up her early retirement and helped save the life of Otto Waddle Jr. High Government Outpost.

Today was now Friday and I was in Zombie Biology dissecting a zombie frog.

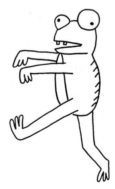

LAME had not shown up in public since the day of the movie. We figured we'd lay low for a while just to be safe. As for LAMER, everyone had a field day with Nerf and what he and his friends had done. For the first time ever the biggest bully in school had lost all support. Nobody was scared of him because what he had done was so . . . well, pathetic. Nerf and the other three just slinked around school trying not to get made fun of.

The fame of LAME was growing. Everyone had posted thousands of pictures and articles about us taking down LAMER and helping the community see the movie.

Even the government wanted in on the fame. They lied about what had happened by telling people that they had enlisted LAME to show the movie at Otto Waddle because they knew that the community would like that.

You still might think it's weird that we would go to so much trouble to save our school. There are days when even I don't understand. But Darth Susan is not someone we want to see emerge victorious. Besides, there is something about being loyal to the mess you are in that makes LAME feel protective of Otto Waddle Jr. High Government Outpost.

I looked around my class and hoped that it was worth it. I saw Mindy, and the two of us smiled at each other.

Yesterday she had complimented me on something, and I had finally said the right thing back.

The speaker on the wall in the classroom crackled to life. Darth Susan had something to say:

As the speaker snapped off we could hear Finn crying,

Trouble in the cafeteria! An angry lizard is rampaging today's lunch options. Who can save us?

I looked at Mindy, she looked at Owen, Owen looked at Xen, and Xen looked at me.

I shut off the lights in our classroom, and under a cloak of darkness, we slipped out and moved into action.

Darth Susan was Darth-pressed and angry. It served her right. She should have known that wherever there is injustice, wherever there is oppression, wherever there is a need for four middle schoolers with mediocre abilities, LAME will be there.